PRAISE FOR TH

'An unmissable series. *Sydney Morning Herald*

'I couldn't put it down. Mark Smith creates this dangerous, lawless new world and manages to champion the decency of youth. Very timely. And what makes it so powerful is that it's frighteningly believable.' Robert Newton

'Mark Smith writes in a taut style that keeps the pages turning... Absorbing entertainment.' *Magpies*

'The superb pacing, natural dialogue, and vivid descriptions of a country and people ravaged by disaster make this a pulse-pounding read.' *Kirkus*

'It's easy to see why Mark Smith's dystopian thriller has been compared with John Marsden's *Tomorrow When the War Began*. I barely came up for breath as the pages flew. So strap yourself in for a high action ride.' *Kids Book Review*

'A riveting story of survival that questions the prices of freedom and safety as well as the value of an individual life...A breakout new series full of romance, danger, and a surprisingly engaging world.' *Kirkus*

'Whenever I put the book down, I felt as if I'd been holding my breath...The world Smith creates is convincing, perhaps because he takes real-world scenarios and kicks them up a notch.' *New Zealand Listener*

'A beautiful and intimate story...Like the best YA fiction, *The Road to Winter* is sure to appeal just as much to an adult audience.' *Otago Daily Times*

'One of those novels that once you start reading, it is nearly impossible to put down again...an unforgettable novel about survival, honour, friendship and love.' *South Coast Register*

'Thought-provoking...insightful and heartbreaking.' *Reading Time*

Mark Smith lives on Victoria's Surf Coast with his family. His first book, *The Road to Winter*, was published in 2016. The second book in the Winter trilogy, *Wilder Country*, won the Indie Book Award—Young Adult, 2018.

LAND OF FENCES

MARK SMITH

TEXT PUBLISHING MELBOURNE AUSTRALIA

textpublishing.com.au

The Text Publishing Company
Swann House
22 William Street
Melbourne Victoria 3000
Australia

Published by The Text Publishing Company, 2019.

Cover and text design by Imogen Stubbs.
Cover images from iStock and Shutterstock.
Typeset by J&M Typesetters.

Printed in Australia by Griffin Press, part of Ovato, an Accredited ISO AS/NZS 14001:2004 Environmental Management System Printer.

ISBN: 9781925773583 (paperback)
ISBN: 9781925774399 (ebook)

A catalogue record for this book is available from the National Library of Australia.

This book is printed on paper certified against the Forest Stewardship Council® Standards. Griffin Press holds FSC chain-of-custody certification SGS-COC-005088. FSC promotes environmentally responsible, socially beneficial and economically viable management of the world's forests.

FSC
www.fsc.org
MIX
Paper from
responsible sources
FSC® C009448

For Albert Johnston Smith
(1927–2017)

1

Kas and I take the track along the clifftops and down to the point. It's another perfect summer day. She's almost running, eager to get to the beach and the rock pools, grabbing my hand and pulling me along. Rowdy is miles ahead of us. He'll be in the water by now.

'Come on! The tide won't wait,' she says over her shoulder.

In the three months since we arrived back in Angowrie, Kas has fallen in love with the sea. She's learnt to swim and surf. She's comfortable dropping off the edge of the reef with me, into the deep waters of the bay. She knows how to prise abalone off the rocks and where to look for crays on the ledges and in the crevices. We compete for who can hold their breath the longest. She's getting better, but I've still got her covered. Years of surfing have taught me how to relax underwater to conserve oxygen.

Now, she laughs and swings around behind me, jumping onto my back. I piggyback her for a few seconds then let her drop her feet to the ground.

'How good is this?' she says. 'Just the two of us and Rowdy and an empty beach.'

'All the beaches are empty remember. And, anyway, we're here to collect food, too,' I say.

The path opens onto the beach at the point. The sand sweeps out towards the reef, where rock pools trap the water from the high tide. It seems like an age ago that we were here with Willow, in the days before Rose died. So much has happened since then—the winter of storms, the journey north into Wilder country, finding Hope and taking her to Harry and Stella in the valley. Then returning to Angowrie to find Ray alive. Kas and I carry the scars—the ones we can see and the ones we can't—to remind us how close we came to losing everything.

This summer we've been able to relax a little. Kas and I hunt and fish and swim and surf, while Ray tends the veggie gardens and helps out skinning the rabbits and cooking meals. It almost seems like a normal life—except we're still on our own here. There have been no more drifters finding their way into our quarantine town and, more importantly, we haven't seen any Wilders since their defeat at the valley farm. Some of them were killed, others fled into the forest and Ramage retreated towards Longley, alone and wounded. We've got no way of knowing if he survived or whether the Wilders have been able to reorganise.

Each day we check the road into town, watching for JT, Daymu and any of the feedstore kids who may have escaped from the No-landers' farm. We figure they would've been here by now if the No-landers had allowed them to leave, as they promised. We both feel a nagging sense of guilt that our escape may have led to them becoming prisoners.

Kas and I have given up wearing clothes at the beach. The summer has turned my skin a deep brown and the sun and saltwater have bleached my hair almost white. Kas is lean and muscled and her black hair is a tangle of knots and braids that fall down her back. I love watching her underwater, her body flexing and rippling in the light when she dives off the point. We're more modest at home with Ray around, wearing shorts and singlets, but each night we lie together with our shoulders touching, skin on skin, salt from our hair crusting the pillow.

Kas leads me out to her favourite pool, a deep sinkhole that hides crabs and sea anemone on its sandy bottom. She dives straight in and surfaces with a smile. She splashes water at Rowdy, who leaps up, trying to snap it out of the air.

'It's so warm this morning,' she says. 'Like a bath.' She duck dives and the water slides over her back and legs. I jump in and follow her down. We'll have to get back to the business of finding food before the tide turns, but for now we can steal half an hour and enjoy ourselves. Straightaway, I know this is one of our breath-holding competitions. Kas sits cross-legged on the sand at the base of the pool, eyes closed, index fingers touching her thumbs, pretending to meditate. Her hair forms a black halo around her head. I ease my way down next to her and wait. Finally, her eyes spring open and she tries to grab me, to push the air out of my lungs. But I'm too quick for her and she strokes for the surface with me at her heels. We burst into the warm blue air and gasp for oxygen.

'Not fair!' she yells. 'I was down there before you.'

'Your mistake, not mine.'

She swims to the edge of the pool and lifts herself onto the rocks. Leaning down to offer me her hand, she pulls me most of the way out before suddenly letting go. I fall back and resurface to hear her laughing.

'You'll never learn, will you?' she says.

I haul myself out and find a flat spot to lie next to her on the rocks. The sun dries us quickly and my skin prickles with little crystals of salt. 'Come on,' I say, getting to my feet. 'Let's get the snorkelling gear and see what we can catch for dinner.'

We fit our masks, and pindrop off the reef. We find the surface, fill our lungs and dive. The summer currents have brought new life to the reef. There are abalone clinging to the rocks, fish of all colours and sizes flitting around just out of reach and the ledges hold crayfish bigger than my forearm. We separate by a few metres and begin to fill our bags, being careful not to take too much. It's a natural foodstore down here, one that has replenished itself in the three years since the virus. It makes me wonder how much better off the planet might be without humans stuffing it up.

Back on the rocks we compare catches. One of my crays has eggs tucked under it so we carefully return it to the water. Kas still marvels at their shells and sharp pincers. 'They're almost too beautiful to eat,' she says.

We make our way to our clothes on the beach. Rowdy struggles to his feet. He's okay once he gets going, but the damage to his hip where he was shot makes it hard for him to get his legs working sometimes. Kas drops to her knees and nuzzles her face into his coat.

'We'd better get back to Ray,' I say.

'Not yet,' she says. 'Let's stay a little bit longer.'

We stretch ourselves out on the sand.

'Do you remember that first day we came down here?' she asks.

'Yeah, of course.' How could I forget? We'd only known each other for a few days but already I was falling for her. And that afternoon we kissed for the first time. 'You and Wils swam in the shallow pool and I dived off the reef.'

'I was so sus of you—this wild boy I could hardly understand.'

I smile. 'When you squatted down next to me to look at the crays I'd bagged, I just wanted to touch you.'

'Ha! I know. I felt it.'

I glance at her and she's looking straight up into the endless sky. She rolls onto her side and lies her hand on my chest. She's mulling something over.

'What is it?' I ask.

She thinks for a while longer then says, 'How long can it go on, Finn?'

'How do you mean?'

'This summer, I've been so...'

'Happy?'

'My life's never been like this. You, me, Ray, Rowdy—we're a family. Is this what it was like for you before the virus?'

'Kinda.'

She lets the conversation sit for a while, but I can tell there's something else eating at her.

'The lights,' she says, at last. 'Do they worry you?'

Since that first night we saw the streetlights flickering, it's happened at least a dozen times, like someone is testing the network.

'Why should it? Remember what the No-landers said about Wentworth, that they were starting to rebuild. The power must be coming from there. That's gotta be good.'

'Not for me,' she says.

'What do you mean?'

She holds up her left hand and runs her fingers over the tracker sitting under the skin.

'It's only streetlights, Kas. They're a long way from being able to track you.'

'If they get a power supply organised who knows what they'll be able to do?'

'We're in a quarantined area. They won't be coming here in a hurry.'

Unconvinced, she avoids eye contact.

We have time for one more swim. The tide is starting to breach the outer reef and before long waves will be swamping the rock pools. We hold hands and jump in, dragging each other to the bottom. Sometimes I make believe we'll swim back to the surface to find the beach crowded with holiday-makers, families with kids lathered in sunscreen and old couples sitting in deckchairs under shade shelters. The smell of barbeques will waft across the beach and someone will have a radio on, listening to the cricket. We'll be forced to do a nude run back to our clothes, while everyone stops and looks and whistles. I don't know why I hang onto these stupid ideas. Maybe it's because I'm afraid of forgetting what life was like before the virus, what a normal day looked like.

Of course, when we climb out there's just Rowdy waiting for us. We pick our way over the reef that's now hot from the sun, dress quickly and make our way into the trees and up the path.

Our bags are bulging with abalone and crays, but I feel guilty for leaving Ray for so long. He's come to the beach with us a couple of times, but he's not interested in going in the water. At most he'll take off his shirt, the deep brown of his sun-struck arms meeting the white skin of his shoulders. As a farmer, he's spent his life hiding from the sun under clothes and hats. 'Buggered if I know why you kids want to expose yourselves to it like you do,' he always says.

Ray is waiting for us in the backyard. He looks excited, pacing up and down, muttering to himself.

'Took your bloody time,' he says. 'Been waitin' ages.'

'What's up?' I ask.

He takes a deep breath. 'You'd better come and see this,' he says.

We leave our dive bags on the porch and follow him to the storage shed. He's spent a lot of time in here recently, making an inventory of our supplies and setting out a plan to ration them. Inside he squeezes past the shelving and stands in front of the workbench. There's a vice bolted to one end and cans of nails and screws line the back wall. And there's an old radio.

'I was muckin' around with this,' he says. He flips the radio over and pulls the back off it. There's a thick tube of batteries. 'We used to listen to these when we were out on the tractors all day, hay baling. I took some batteries out of the torch in the kitchen.' He settles the radio on the bench and pulls a retractable aerial from the top. He turns and looks at us. 'Now listen,' he says.

He pushes the switch on the side and begins fiddling with the tuning dial. At first there's just static, white noise from nowhere. But then, a voice that sounds like it's coming from a million miles away, low and hard to hear. We lean closer and Ray turns the volume up as high as it will go.

'This is government radio 3HST, broadcasting from the Central Coordination Zone. A critical service announcement will be made by the Regional Director at 1900 hours.'

The message repeats, over and over.

2

'How will we know when it's seven o'clock?' Kas is agitated.

I take her hand and weave my fingers into hers. 'Don't get too excited,' I say, though I can't think of any logical reason not to—things might have progressed further than the No-landers knew.

'Seven in the evening. It shouldn't be too hard to work out,' Ray says. We've moved to the kitchen and he's set the radio on the table, handling it like it's some sort of sacred object. 'We're about two-thirds of the way through summer, I reckon, so seven would be an hour before sunset.'

We've become used to living without time. My old life before the virus was ruled by it—what time to get up, catch the bus, arrive at school, move between classes, come home, surf, eat, sleep. Now the sun and moon tell us everything we need to know. We go to bed with the dark and get up with the light.

Waiting for the broadcast, the rest of the day seems to drag. In the afternoon, Kas and I shell the abalone and tenderise them with the hammer. We put the crays in a tank with sea-water bucketed over from the beach. Kas is quiet, and there's not much I can say to reassure her. At dinner, she moves her abalone around the plate. Ray has cooked them up in garlic and chillies from the garden. It's her favourite meal but she barely touches it.

We don't want to waste the batteries, but we can't miss the broadcast either, so we turn the radio on after we've finished eating. The same message is playing. Kas pushes her chair away from the table and walks out onto the porch.

She has her back against the railing, her arms hugging her chest. 'Can't stand this,' she says. 'I'm gonna take Yogi for a ride along the beach.'

'What?' I can't believe what I'm hearing. 'You don't want to listen to the broadcast? Why?'

'Because it'll change everything. It'll change us, you and me,' she says.

'You're guessing, Kas.'

'Come on, Finn. They're reorganising. They've got power and radio. How long until they reach Angowrie? And then what happens to me?'

'Even if—and that's a big if—they get someone down here,

the whole Siley situation could've changed.' I know I'm making this up, but I'm looking for any argument to make her feel better.

She shakes her head, walks down the steps, lifts the bridle from its hook by the shed door and disappears through the sheoaks towards the paddock on Parker Street. There's no point following her. She'll slip onto Yogi's back and canter him along the riverbank. With the tide high, she won't have a lot of beach to ride on, but she'll do laps until Yogi's exhausted.

'Finn,' Ray calls from the kitchen.

I sit opposite him at the table. The repeated message has stopped, replaced by metallic beeps at regular intervals.

Then it starts. The reception fades in and out and Ray and I strain to hear what's being said above the static. After about ten minutes, there's silence. Ray flicks the switch and we sit looking at each other across the table.

Our part of the country has been divided into coordination zones, each with a hub at its centre. We're in the western zone and Wentworth is our hub. But there are also satellite towns in each zone—and Longley is in ours.

The only time Angowrie is mentioned is when quarantined areas are listed. No one is allowed to enter them and, while survivors from other areas are encouraged to try to get to their nearest hub, people in quarantined zones are told to stay put until further notice.

'What do you make of all that?' Ray asks.

'Pretty light on detail,' I say. 'Nothing about what's happening in places like Wentworth, no mention of how many people have survived or whether any sort of government's been set up. Nothing about the virus either.'

'And nothing about Sileys,' he says.

'Do you reckon that's good, or bad?'

'I've got no idea, son. It all sounds pretty sketchy and it's hard to tell if that's deliberate or not. It kind of depends on who it is making the broadcasts.'

'The message this arvo said it was government radio.'

'Could be anybody saying that, though.'

It's a beautiful, still evening outside. The sun slants into the yard from the west, catching the yellow tips on the sheoaks, making them glow like firesticks. At the beach, I sit on the platform to watch Kas riding Yogi in the shallows. She has him at a trot and the spray rises in little explosions as his hooves hit the water. She looks so comfortable on his back, like she's part of him. I remember the first conversation in the kitchen with Rose when she told me about watching Kas escape from Swan's Marsh. Kas was just a distant figure on horseback but Rose knew it was her by the way she rode.

When they reach the river mouth, it's flowing deep with the tide so Kas wheels Yogi around to come back. Now she urges him into a canter, her body leaning forward, her face close to his mane. I walk down onto the sand and wait for them to turn again at the rocks below the cliffs. Kas brings him round in a wide arc and lets him slow his pace.

Yogi is blowing hard and sweat glistens on his flanks. Kas pulls him to a halt but stays on his back.

'So?' she says.

'Why don't you come home, and Ray and I'll try to make sense of it with you.'

'Tell me now,' she demands.

'At least get off Yogi. I can't see you properly. The sun's behind you.'

She gives Yogi a nudge with her heels and brings him around so they're facing into the sun.

'Shit, you're stubborn,' I say.

She doesn't say anything, just tucks her hair behind her ears and waits.

I fill her in on everything we heard in the broadcast. I have to talk over Yogi's breathing and the regular crashing of the waves on the bar. Kas listens in silence, her eyes locked on mine.

When I'm finished, she shifts on Yogi's back and looks out towards the point. 'See,' she says. 'Everything is going to change.'

'We don't know that. There was nothing about Sileys.'

'That's worse,' she says. 'It means Sileys are still slaves. They'll hunt me down.'

'They might not be able to do that. We don't even know how many people have survived in Wentworth.'

'We know how many have survived in Longley. And who do you think they're going to put in charge there? Ramage or Tusker?'

I don't know what to say.

Her voice is tired, resigned. 'They're going to rely on people who know the country, the ones who've kept the farms going—and the ones who've got experience hunting Sileys. Wilders.'

I don't let on, but what she says makes sense. They probably can't afford to be choosy about who they put in charge of the satellite towns.

'Come on,' I say. 'Let's go home.' I reach my hand up to her. She looks at me for a few seconds then pulls me up behind her. She nudges Yogi again and we ride towards the river mouth, then along the bank where it cuts through the dunes. I hold her loosely around the waist. Her back is wet with perspiration.

'What am I going to do?' she says so quietly I can't tell whether she's talking to me or to herself. 'Finn?'

'You mean what are *we* going to do?' I say. 'What we've always done: sit tight, keep watch, be ready to run if we have to.'

'You've got no reason to run. They're not going to try to capture you. You'll be a hero—the boy that survived for three years. They'll love that story.'

'And what if it's Ramage or Tusker who come looking? I don't reckon they're going to call me a hero.'

We reach the paddock halfway up Parker Street where I buried the Wilder, the one Rose killed. Kas swings her leg over Yogi's neck and drops to her feet. I slide off and Kas undoes the bridle. There's no need to tie him up or fence him in; he knows there's feed here and that Kas isn't far away.

'I'm so tired,' Kas says, leaning into me. 'Can we spare the water for a bath?'

We've had some good downpours through the summer so the tanks are well stocked. 'Sure,' I say, happy to have something else to talk about. It's almost dark by the time we walk through to the house. The smell of garlic and abalone hangs in the kitchen. There's no sign of Ray, which isn't unusual—he goes to bed early. Rowdy stirs on his blanket in the corner, gets to his feet and stretches.

We fill all the pots we have with water and put them on the stove to heat. Ray is confident we've got enough gas to last for years if we use it wisely.

Kas runs a little cold water into the bath and I bring the pots in one by one. It's not very hot and it only allows for a shallow bath but once a month we treat ourselves like this, when our skin is crusty with dry salt and our hair is matted like rope. We usually take it in turns, topping up with warm water in between. But tonight Kas takes my hand when I go to leave. She pulls me close and undresses me, then peels her own clothes off. I sit behind her in the bath and she leans back into my arms.

'Wash my hair?' she asks.

We have bars of laundry soap Dad used to sell at the hardware. They're a foot long and you can cut off whatever size you need. It's pretty harsh stuff but it cleans well.

I take one of the pots and pour water over Kas's head while she leans forward. Then I go to work with the soap, pushing my fingers into her scalp and pulling them through the knots.

Kas moans, low and soft.

The smell of the soap begins to replace her hair's usual musty odour. I rinse it again and again.

'Do you ever wish…' she says

'What?' I ask.

'That you could stop time—hold it for a while so you don't have to worry about what the future holds?'

'I don't want to stop time. I want to go back in time,' I say.

'Back to when? What would you do?'

'Back to before the virus,' I say, 'when I lived with Mum and Dad. I'd tell them every day that I loved them. I'd spend more time with them. I'd slow down instead of always rushing.'

She stays quiet for a while then.

'What about you,' I ask. 'What would you do?'

She doesn't hesitate. 'I'd go back to the day Rose and I got separated at Swan's Marsh, when we escaped from Ramage. I'd wait where she told me.' She hugs her arms to her chest and rests her head on her knees. 'I should have been there for her. I shouldn't have left her. I could have looked out for her. Everything that happened to her was my fault.'

I rest my forehead against her back. 'No, it wasn't, Kas. None of it was your fault.'

I climb out of the bath, dry myself and pass the towel to her. Her eyes are rimmed with tears. She stands up and I wrap her in the towel. 'Come on,' I say. 'Let's go to bed.'

We've been sleeping together most of the summer. It happened more by necessity at the start—we had to make space for Ray, which meant me giving up my room. I could've slept on the couch but Kas wouldn't let me. We were spending so much time together, the nights just seemed like an extension of the days. Still, it felt weird, almost like we knew each other too well—we'd argued and made up a hundred times, fought and survived the Wilders.

We found condoms all over town—in bathrooms and under beds. They were the last things people were thinking of when they took off to escape the virus.

The first time was amazing and scary and exciting all at the same time. The last two years had forced us to be suspicious of everyone, and I don't think either of us knew how to let our defences down completely. But experience had taught us that of all the people left in the world, this person here was the one we could trust the most.

3

The sound is unmistakable—a whistle. High pitched. Human.

We're in the backyard, skinning rabbits. Rowdy cocks his ears and growls. Kas and I swing around and look at Ray, who's standing on the porch. 'That way,' he says, pointing towards the river.

We push the rabbits back into our hunting bag and scan the backyard for anything that might give us away. The shed door creaks in the wind. I shut it and follow Ray and Kas into the house. We pull down blinds and close windows. Then we sit and wait at the kitchen table.

The whistle comes again. It sounds different this time,

twisted by the wind.

'What'd you think?' Kas says.

'I think we should check it out,' I say.

Ray takes hold of Rowdy by the collar to stop him following. 'Be careful,' he says. 'Don't do anything stupid.'

I open the back door a fraction and check the yard. It's clear. We stick to the cover of the trees behind the houses leading down to the river.

'We should have brought the rifle,' Kas says.

'We're only checking it out, remember. We're not going to give ourselves away.'

At the last house, we leave the trees and make a dash for the low fence that faces the river. Clumps of moonah trees dot the open area along the bank where the Wilders camped last year. Everything looks normal. There's no sign of anyone.

'They might've moved on—passed through like the drifters last spring,' I say. But I barely get the words out when Kas grabs my arm and pulls me back down.

'I saw something,' she says. 'Behind the trees to the right.'

We have our backs to the fence when the whistle comes again, closer this time. I climb to my knees and chance a look over the top. She's right, there's something moving behind the trees. Something big.

The whistle comes again. Then, 'Finn? Kas?' It's a girl's voice.

Daymu appears from behind the trees, followed by JT, who's leading Black Bess by the reins. They wave and stagger towards us. We run across the road and pull up short of them. They look exhausted, thin and covered in cuts and scratches. JT has a bandage tied around his head and blood seeps through above his ear. Daymu leans heavily on a stick.

'Is there anyone else with you?' I ask, looking back towards the shops. I'm happy to see them but instinct makes me cautious.

'No,' JT says. 'We're on our own.'

'You're not being followed?'

'No.'

Kas helps Daymu while I loop JT's arm around my shoulder to support him. We make our way slowly up the street to the front of our place. Black Bess follows. I call to Ray when we reach the backyard and he comes out to help. We get Daymu and JT inside and sit them at the table.

'Jesus,' Ray says. 'You two look like you've been through the wars.'

JT and Daymu stare at him. I do the introductions. JT can only nod his head. 'You got any food?' he asks, his voice strained.

We've got some leftover stew from last night. Ray heats it on the stove. Daymu stares at the flame. 'Gas,' I say, and she half-smiles.

'What's happened to you?' Kas asks. 'Where are the others? Did you escape?'

Ray interrupts. 'Food first.'

'Yeah,' JT says. 'Food would be good.'

'There's not much here,' Ray says. 'Just leftovers, but we'll have a proper meal later.'

They eat, hunched over their bowls and slurping loudly.

Daymu apologises. 'We haven't had proper food in ages. Just berries and mushrooms we found along the way.'

They've been living rough. Their clothes are matted in dirt and sweat and their hands are almost black. Both have grass and twigs in their hair and their lips are a mess of sores. JT leans back and burps loudly, which makes us all laugh.

Kas has been watching them closely, too. 'Let's get you two cleaned up,' she says. 'Finn, hot water. Ray, bandages and antiseptic cream. I'm going to run the bath.'

Daymu and JT hold hands while we work around them. I put the water on to heat and head out into the yard to find Black Bess. She's grazing on the grass at the base of the water tank. I lead her through to Yogi's paddock. They check each other out before going back to eating.

In the house, Kas and Daymu are in the bathroom with the door shut. After a few minutes Kas calls me to bring warm water. Daymu is hunched over in the bath and there are bruises all over her shoulders and back. Kas takes the pot and shoos me out the door.

JT is still at the table, his chin resting in his hands. 'It's so good to see you,' he says. 'I didn't think we were going to make it.'

Ray stands behind him and puts his hand on JT's shoulder. 'There's plenty of time, son. Don't knock yourself out.'

'You have to hear what's happened,' he says, turning to me. 'We're safe here for the time being, but...'

'So you *were* followed?' I ask.

'No, we weren't. But even if we were, that'd be the least of our problems.'

Kas sticks her head out of the bathroom. 'Don't start without me,' she says.

Daymu emerges then, wrapped in a towel. She limps heavily and supports herself against the doorframe. 'It's only a sprained ankle,' she says. Kas shepherds her into our room. When they come out Daymu is wearing some of Kas's clothes and her ankle is bandaged.

'You're next,' Kas says to JT. 'But I'm guessing you won't want me to help you in there.' She smiles.

JT struggles to his feet. 'I haven't had a bath in two years,' he says. 'But I reckon I can look after myself.'

Half an hour later we are all sitting at the kitchen table. Daymu and JT look a little better now that they're clean and they've had something to eat. The cut above JT's ear has been washed. There's a chunk of hair missing and the scalp shows through. He touches the wound with his fingertips and winces.

It's mid-afternoon by now. Ray has two rabbits cooking in a big pot on the stove. Their gamey smell fills the house. Daymu's eyes wander around the kitchen, taking it all in. 'No wonder you wanted to get back here,' she says. 'Can't believe you've got gas.'

'What happened after we left the No-landers' farm,' I ask.

Kas and I escaped with Hope from the No-landers' farm last spring. We didn't want any part of their guerilla war with the Wilders. Tahir was dangerous and unpredictable.

JT looks around the room, as though he's trying to get the details in order before starting. 'Tahir was fuming,' he says, finally. 'He tried to get a shot at you when you took off, but Danka stood in front of him and he ended up shooting into the air.'

'Danka!' Kas says. 'Is she okay? Where is she?'

'I'll get to that,' JT says, but something in his voice tells us the news isn't good.

'The hunting party returned later that morning. Tahir had herded all of us into the machinery shed and locked the door. We were prisoners again. We heard them arguing in the yard, fighting among themselves. There was a gap in the wall where the iron had rusted through. Tahir was screaming at Afa and Kaylo, the two No-landers he accused of letting you escape. Afa backed off but Kaylo gave as good as he got. But he was unarmed. He pushed Tahir too far.' JT breaks off and looks to Daymu.

'Tahir shot him,' she says. 'Just like that.' She snaps her fingers.

'You mean he killed him?' Kas's eyes are wide.

Daymu nods.

Kas and I can add this to the list of things we're responsible for.

JT continues. 'Even Tahir seemed shocked at what he'd done. It was one thing to kill Wilders, but Kaylo was a No-lander, like him.

'In the afternoon, we smelled smoke and meat cooking. After dark, the door was unlocked and Gabriel told us all to come out into the yard. We'd seen what happen to Kaylo, so we were shit-scared. All the No-landers were in Tahir's house and Gabriel took us inside. Tahir sat at the head of the table. It was covered with plates of kangaroo meat. The atmosphere was weird, like nothing had happened that afternoon. Afa sat off to the side, and everyone was eyeing the food.'

The mention of food reminds Ray to check on the stew. He takes a knife and starts to break up the rabbits.

'What happened then?' Kas asks.

'We ate,' Daymu says. 'We didn't feel good about it but we were starving and most us hadn't tasted meat in months. Tahir encouraged us, moving around the table and boasting about how he'd provide as much food as we wanted if we stayed with him. I hate to say it but, right then, I didn't care what I had to do to stay fed. I reckon most of us felt the same way.'

'He was bribing you,' I say.

'Yeah, and we knew it,' JT says. 'I looked at Danka. She nodded her head and kept eating. Whatever happened from there on, we'd need our strength.'

'There's no shame in that,' Ray says, standing in front of the stove.

JT continues. 'Tahir gave this big speech about how everyone had to work together—Sileys, No-landers and the feedstore kids. But he said there was only one way that was going to happen—we'd have to fight. He talked about organising raiding parties to steal food from the farms around Longley, hitting them at night then retreating to the valley.'

'He made it sound almost attractive,' Daymu says. 'You know what he's like, with all his talk about bravery and having to stand up for ourselves. But then his voice changed. His smile disappeared and he started talking about discipline, like we were some sort of army. And he warned us about what would happen if anyone broke his rules. He didn't mention Kaylo but we all knew what he meant.'

Ray has lined up the bowls on the bench by the stove and now he ladles the thick stew into them. Daymu and JT break off their story to watch. They remind me of how Harry and the valley farmers looked after last winter when they'd worked for the Wilders—drawn and lean and hungry. There's so much more we need to know, but for now they've got to regain their strength.

I light two candles and set them on the table. The kitchen seems to close in around us, the little buds of light reflecting in the windows.

There'll be no leftovers this time. We eat until we're full. Ray sits at the head of the table. 'We don't want to press you too hard,' he says to JT and Daymu. 'But we need to know if we're safe here, at least for the time being. Can you tell us any more?'

'I'm okay,' JT says.

'Me too,' Daymu says. 'And thanks for the food. Kas told us you were a great cook.'

'What happened after the meal in Tahir's house?' Ray asks.

'The next few days were spent organising work parties for the farm,' Daymu says. 'But it was pretty clear we'd be doing all the work. In the meantime, the No-landers hunted and kept us supplied with meat. They didn't lock us up at night anymore— and we had more food—but we still felt like prisoners.'

'How long did this go on?' Kas asks.

'A couple of months, I reckon,' JT says. 'Tahir hardly came out of his house. Gabriel was different, though. He never let on, but I got the feeling he was turning against Tahir. A few times we heard arguments, shouting and swearing.'

'How did you two escape?' Kas asks.

'We had a burst of hot weather—too hot to work in the paddocks,' JT says. 'We were lying around in the shed when we heard shots coming from the valley entrance. Before we could move, the door slid shut and we were locked in again.'

'There were about a dozen Wilders,' Daymu says, 'led by Tusker. The No-landers took off up the ridge into the forest. They left us for dead.'

Daymu bites her lip then continues. 'The Wilders found us easily enough. Herded us out into the yard. Tusker had this big leering grin on his face. He kept asking about you, Kas. He was so pissed off you weren't there.'

A little shudder passes through Kas and she squeezes her hands tight between her knees.

'It was bad enough we'd been caught again,' Daymu continues, 'but we hadn't heard the worst of it.'

'The worst of it?' I say. 'What could be worse?'

Daymu looks at Kas. 'Have you heard what's been happening in Wentworth? And Longley?' she says.

'You mean the coordination zones? The satellite towns?' Kas says, her voice flat. She tells them about the broadcast on the radio.

Daymu nods. 'Each area has a commissioner,' she says.

I know what's coming. My stomach twists in a knot and I feel the stew rise in the back of my throat.

'Ramage is alive,' JT says, the words cutting me like knives. 'He's Longley's commissioner.'

'And Tusker?' Kas asks.

'His deputy,' JT replies.

4

The conversation Kas and I had on the beach rings in my head. She was right—this summer has been an illusion. We've been lulled into thinking we're okay, but the real world is pressing in on us again. And, if it's possible, Ramage is even more dangerous now.

JT and Daymu are tired. They desperately need to sleep.

'There's so much more we need to tell you,' JT says. 'But can it wait till morning?'

'Course it can,' Ray says. 'There's an old mattress out in the shed we'll bring in for you. And we've got blankets.'

Daymu struggles to her feet, leaning against the table. 'I'm sorry,' she says. 'We didn't know where else to go.'

Kas puts her arm around her shoulder. 'You're welcome here,' she says. 'We Sileys have to stick together.'

Daymu forces a smile.

JT and I go out to the shed. He looks weary to his bones. As we struggle out the door with the mattress he stops. 'Thanks, mate,' he says, too tired to say anything more.

'Kas is right,' I say. 'We've gotta stick together.'

Once Daymu and JT have closed the door on the lounge room and Ray has headed to bed, Kas and I sit either side of the one candle left burning on the table. The flame lights her face, highlighting her birthmark.

'I can't stop thinking about Hope,' she says. 'Ramage'll know where to find her.'

'Harry and Stella will protect her,' I say.

'But what if they can't? Ramage can do what he likes now and he'll take her back. She's a Siley's daughter.'

I don't have an answer for her, except that there's nothing we can do about it right now.

'I can't believe the authorities in Wentworth have put Ramage in charge of Longley,' I say.

'Maybe they're as bad as he is. This country they're trying to rebuild wasn't fair to begin with, so why should it be fair now?'

I don't sleep well—and I'm pretty sure Kas doesn't either. The wind moans through the sheoaks and the cypress scrapes the spout outside our window. I toss and turn, and when I finally sleep I dream of Ramage turning his back and taunting me to shoot him as he mounts his trailbike and disappears into the night.

In the morning Kas and I find JT sitting on the back step, trying to bandage the wound above his ear.

'You're doing a shit job,' I say, and he laughs. I take the bandage and wind it firmly around his head before tying it off.

Daymu watches through the open doorway. She looks better after a night's sleep. 'You want to eat out here?' she asks.

Ray has provided the eggs and dipped into the stores for one of the remaining cans of beans.

'Yeah, out here,' Kas says.

We sit cross-legged around a frying pan of tomato omelette and a pot of beans. Ray struggles down the steps, carrying a chair from the kitchen. 'All right for you lot,' he says. 'I'd have to break my ankles to sit like that.'

There's not enough food to fill us, but I'll check the traps later in the morning. When we're finished, JT moves over to the shed, sitting with his back to the wall. Daymu follows, while Kas and I sit on what's left of the grass in the yard.

There's a tension in the air that Kas, Ray and I haven't felt all summer. It's the same house and yard, the same river flowing out to the beach, and the same waves breaking across the bar—but the news Daymu and JT have brought has changed everything. The radio broadcast was unsettling, especially for Kas, but I still had a sense time was on our side. We were quarantined and protected by our isolation, and the storms had made travel almost impossible. But the world beyond Angowrie is rebuilding quicker than I'd thought—and the more organised it gets, the more danger we are in.

'So,' I say. 'What happened after the Wilders arrived at the No-landers' farm? How did you escape?'

JT crosses his arms and leans back in the sun. 'Tusker was beside himself when he saw Daymu and Danka.'

'Sileys,' Kas says.

Daymu digs her toes into the dirt. 'There's a bounty on every Siley they catch,' JT says. 'They hold them at Longley until someone comes from Wentworth to collect them.'

'What sort of bounty?' I ask.

'Sheep, cattle, grain. They see it as win–win. Wentworth gets Sileys and the farms can start working again to provide food.'

'What happens to the Sileys at Wentworth?' Kas asks.

'We don't know,' Daymu says. 'We only discovered this much because a Wilder got drunk and started talking. That's how we found out about Ramage, too.'

'What did they say about him?' I ask.

'A whole lot of stuff you don't want to hear. Somehow he made it back to Longley. They reckon he nearly died. He can't travel, but he trusts Tusker to act for him.'

'Good luck with that,' I say. 'Trust and Tusker aren't two words I'd use in the same sentence.'

'How long were you held at the farm?' Ray asks, leaning forward with his elbows on his knees.

'A couple of days,' JT says. 'Tusker didn't want to risk leaving any of his men in case the No-landers came back. On the third morning, they tied us in pairs and marched us out the gate.'

'Where were the No-landers?' Kas asks.

'Out there somewhere,' Daymu says. 'We heard them signalling to each other across the valley.'

'Two high-pitched whistles answered by three the same?' I say.

'You know it?' JT says.

'Yeah. We heard it when they followed us to Longley last spring.'

'We didn't even get out of the valley before they attacked,' JT continues. 'It was crazy. Shots fired. Everyone running. The Wilders took cover in the trees, pulling Danka and the feedstore kids along with them. It was the Sileys they wanted, but Daymu and I were too quick for them. We were tied together but we ran towards the farmhouse. When we got there we worked free of our ties and took off into the bush on Bess.'

'That's rough country,' I say. 'Steep and rocky. No place to be riding a horse.'

'We didn't get far,' Daymu says, 'but we were safe. We'd put enough distance between us and the Wilders.'

'It took us two days to find our way out to the Swan's Marsh road,' JT says. 'There was no sign of anyone—Wilders or No-landers. We were starving, but we decided the best bet was to try to get through to the coast.' He stops and pushes his legs underneath him so he's squatting against the wall. 'We got lost,' he says. 'We ate berries, ferns, anything we could hold down. I lost count of the number of times we spewed.'

'So, you never saw anyone? No one tried to follow you?' Kas asks.

'There were some drifters on the road near Pinchgut Junction, but they were headed towards Swan's Marsh,' JT says.

'They won't find any shelter there,' I say. 'Not if the Monahans catch sight of them.'

The sun is fully up now and it filters through the trees into the backyard. There are decisions to be made, but even if we need to leave Angowrie, JT and Daymu won't be fit to travel for a few days. And right at the moment I can't think of anywhere safer than where we are. We know the terrain here, where to hide, all the escape routes.

JT seems happy to talk, so I ask him how he came to be at the feedstore last year.

He eases down and sits against the wall. 'My mum died when I was little, so it was just me and Dad on the farm.' He looks uncomfortable, picking at a seam on his shorts. 'I never knew what Dad did. He'd disappear for days at a time and leave me on my own.'

'What are you talking about?' Kas turns her head to the side, trying to follow JT.

He can't look at her. 'Dad was a driver with—'

We're all leaning forward now. Only Daymu is unmoved. She squeezes JT's arm, coaxing him to speak.

'He transported Sileys,' JT says, his eyes locked on the ground at his feet.

'He did *what*?' Kas says, her voice low, accusing.

'I didn't know,' JT says. 'Honestly, Kas. He never spoke about it.'

'So how did you find out?' she demands.

'There was paperwork left in the truck one day. I saw it. There were names, delivery dates. I asked him and he said it was the only work he could get.' He hesitates. 'I'm sorry.'

Kas looks straight at JT, and all I see is pity in her eyes. 'Don't beat yourself up about it. You've stuck with Daymu and helped Finn and me escape.'

There's a pause and I take the opportunity to change the subject. 'But how did you end up being captured and held at the feedstore? What happened to your dad?' I ask.

JT turns his face away and I realise he's swiping away a tear. Daymu loops her arm through his and pulls him close.

'He killed himself,' JT says. He leaves a long silence while we take this in. We look at each other, hardly daring to breathe.

'I found him,' JT says. 'In the shed. I had to cut him down. I had to bury him. I had to forget he ever existed.'

'It doesn't mean he didn't love you, son,' Ray says. His voice sounds old and steady and tired.

'Maybe,' JT says. 'But there was no note, no nothing. He left me on my own. That's a pretty strange kind of love.'

'Adults sometimes have reasons for doing things they don't think they can share. I know it's not fair,' Ray says.

JT sits quietly for a while. Rowdy moves between us, angling for a pat. We all want the distraction, and he gets the affection he's looking for.

'Anyway,' JT says finally, 'it wasn't long before Ramage's men moved out onto the plains and started rounding up anybody they could find. I was dumb—trying to work the farm on my own, instead of running.'

'How long ago was this?' Kas asks.

'I'm not sure,' he says. 'But you and Rose had escaped by the time I got to the feedstore. I remember how angry Ramage was. He made us all come out into the yard while he tied Ken Butler to a rope and dragged him behind the trailbike.'

It's strange, this piecing together of our lives, all the connections and near misses. Rose had told me about Ken Butler being dragged into the Monahan's yard at Swan's Marsh, how she wished she'd never seen it.

'We must have just missed each other,' Kas says. 'Ken was killed because he helped us escape.'

The next few days are spent hunting, fishing and eating while JT and Daymu regain their strength. We could survive like this for as long as we're left alone, but there's a shadow over everything we do. We post sentries on the ridge above the football ground, taking it in turns to watch the road. There've been no drifters or Wilders, but the bounty on the heads of Sileys will be enough to bring hunting parties from the north. They'll fight their way through the storm damage into quarantined areas like ours to get here before the authorities. And Ramage and Tusker will be their own lawmakers, out to settle old scores. We know they'll come, we just don't know when.

5

I like sentry duty, looking out over what remains of Angowrie.
Every time I come up here, it seems a little bit different, like
the bush has moved closer to the buildings, reaching out to
reclaim the town. The roads are only half the width they used
to be; the asphalt has been lifted and buckled by the roots of
trees and the grass has spread into the cracks.

I find a comfy spot with a view of the road, my back against
a weathered stringybark and my legs stretched out in front.
Rowdy settles next to me, resting his nose in my lap, knowing
I'll scratch him behind the ears.

The noise is distant at first, a scraping sound followed by

the thrum of an engine. It gradually gets louder, coming along the road into town. The scraping stops, but the motor revs then drops to an idle, and there's just the rumble of a diesel engine pushing through the trees.

I'm on my feet and running. I sprint down the hill towards the bridge, Rowdy racing ahead. My heart is in my mouth and my breath comes in short gasps. I haven't had to move this fast in months and my legs feel slow. By the time we make the bridge, the scraping has started up again, the heavy sound of metal on bitumen and the slaving of the engine behind it.

Kas calls to me as I run along the riverbank. She's with JT and Daymu, hiding behind a cypress hedge in the house next to the petrol station. I veer towards them and dive for cover. Rowdy almost lands on top of me.

'What is it?' Kas asks. She's climbed into the hedge and stuck her head through to get a better view of the road.

'Dunno,' I say. 'I couldn't see it from the ridge.'

The rest of us pull ourselves up next to her, our eyes fixed on the bridge. JT has the rifle, and he slides the bolt back to load it.

The sound is louder now, filling the valley. Finally we see it—a big army truck with a bulldozer blade on the front. It stops on the bridge and the driver lifts the blade from the road. As far as we can tell, there's just the one vehicle. It edges forward now, and turns parallel to the river, coming towards us. Kas has hold of my arm. I look down to Rowdy and point my finger. He drops to the ground.

'Where's Ray?' I whisper.

'At home,' Kas replies.

The truck slows about twenty metres from us, then turns and reverses over the gutter and up onto the grass of the riverbank. Exhaust fumes fill the air. Other than Ramage's trail bike, we haven't seen any sort of vehicle for three years, and the size and noise of it is surreal, an assault on our senses. The driver kills the motor. Then the passenger door swings open and a soldier in full fatigues steps out. He carries a machine gun and a mask covers his face. He hits the side of the truck and half a dozen soldiers, all dressed the same, spill out the back. It's quiet enough to hear the thuds as their boots hit the ground. The driver hasn't moved, but a crackling noise comes from a loudspeaker mounted on the roof of the cabin.

The male voice is harsh and metallic. 'All survivors, please show yourselves.' He repeats this message at least five times, adding '*Now!*' at the end.

We're frozen in our positions, buried in the hedge, but keeping the truck in view.

'You are in a quarantined zone,' the voice continues. 'We are here to evacuate you. Show yourselves.' The soldiers surround the truck, sweeping left and right with their guns.

The voice repeats the announcement over and over, the sound echoing up the valley and bouncing back at us, garbling the words. Finally, the driver opens his door and climbs down. He's not in uniform, but he is wearing a mask too. There's something familiar about the way he moves, his shoulders hunched towards his ears and his legs splayed. He walks around the front of the truck and talks to the first soldier, who seems to be giving the orders. They're arguing, though we can't make out what they're saying. The driver's arms wave in the air, pointing to the ridge then towards the river mouth. The soldier turns and barks orders at the others, who lower their weapons and begin to climb back into the truck. He then reaches into the cabin and pulls out some sheets of paper in plastic sleeves. He pushes them at the driver and directs him to the power pole by the side of the road, only a few metres from where we're hiding. The driver opens a metal box on the truck's side and lifts out a hammer, before walking towards us and nailing a sheet to the pole. He's close enough for us to hear his laboured breathing through the mask. Then he walks along the road attaching sheets to two other power poles, before lumbering back to the truck.

All the soldiers are inside now. The driver stops at his door and scans the town one more time. Before he mounts the steps he pulls the mask from his face. His beard is longer and more grizzled, but the scar down the side of his face is unmistakable.

It's Tusker.

The truck throbs to life and Tusker grinds through the gears. He drives a hundred metres to the car park below the lookout, where he turns in a wide arc and comes back past us. The truck doesn't stop again as it crosses the bridge and heads up the hill and out of town.

We stay where we are until the sound of the engine has faded into the distance. JT climbs out the front of the hedge, checks both ways then walks to the notice on the nearest power pole.

We all follow. The print is faded and hard to read, as though the printer was low on ink. JT reads it aloud:

> 'Compulsory Evacuation Order. Towns in this area fall under the jurisdiction of the South West Regional Commissioner. Any survivors within this zone must report to the quarantine transition camp at Longley, where health services are provided. Decontamination teams are coming to your area. Survivors who have not voluntarily evacuated will be detained and transported to Longley. Anyone found to be harbouring Sileys will be arrested and charged. In the interest of public health, it is your duty to comply with this order.'

He hesitates, turns to look at us, and continues. 'By order, B. Ramage. Commissioner. South West Region.'

We all stare at the notice. The edges flap in the breeze.

Without another word, we turn and head back to the house. Ray meets us in the driveway. His hands are pushed deep into his pockets and his hat sits low over his forehead.

'You heard?' I say.

'Yeah,' he replies. 'Recognise any of them?'

'Tusker.'

'Shit,' he says.

We file into the kitchen. I can hardly bear to look at Kas. Her head is down and she is rubbing the palm of her hand into her forehead. I know what she's thinking—that harbouring

Sileys is a crime and we're all implicated.

'Why the masks?' JT says.

'They think it's a contaminated area,' I say.

'Nah,' JT replies. 'There's something else going on. Did the Wilders ever wear masks when they came to Angowrie?'

'No,' I say, and a creeping dread works its way into my gut.

'Maybe they're being cautious,' Ray says. 'Or—'

'Or what?' Kas says, her voice barely a whisper.

'Or the virus is mutating. They don't have control of it.'

No one speaks. The enormity of what we've seen this morning is beginning to sink in. This is our worst nightmare: the Wilders and the army working together.

Kas sits next to Daymu. Their shoulders touch. 'We're the problem,' Kas says. 'We're the ones they're after.'

There's anger in JT's voice. 'Don't start down that track, Kas. Don't even go there. We're all in this together.'

Kas smiles. 'Thanks, mate,' she says. It's the first time I've heard her call anyone *mate* and the word sounds strange coming from her. 'But you've gotta be realistic. You three,'—she nods her head at Ray, JT and me—'you'll be in enough trouble without making it worse by trying to hide Daymu and me.'

Ray leans back in his chair and crosses his arms. 'What do we know for sure?' he asks.

We fill him in on the notice nailed to the pole.

'We have to be gone before the decontamination squads get here,' Daymu says. Her voice sounds small and defeated.

'Who do you mean by *we*?' I ask.

Daymu nods at Kas. 'Us,' she says. 'Regardless of what

anyone else decides to do, we have to run. We can't be here when they arrive.'

'Run where?' JT says.

'The truck didn't continue on down the coast road,' Daymu says. 'Why not? Why didn't they go through to the other towns?'

I hadn't thought about that. 'The next town is Lewtas Bay,' I say. 'About forty kilometres. When the virus hit, no one came from that direction—they must have headed inland.'

'To where?' Kas asks.

'I'm not sure, but I'm guessing the road would lead to the smaller towns west of Longley.'

'What are you getting at?' Ray asks.

I think I see where Daymu is coming from. 'It's easier to clear the inland route to Lewtas Bay from Longley, so all the coast between here and there is being left, at least for now.'

Kas has perked up. 'What's the country like along the coast?' she asks.

'There's not much there, mostly cliffs and rocky points but there are little pockets of houses where a couple of creeks come out. The road drops to sea level, crosses the creeks then climbs back up into the forest.'

'How far?' Daymu asks.

'The closest one is Megs Creek, about twenty-five k's.'

'And what's there?'

'Maybe a dozen houses.'

Megs was one of those places you drove through without realising—quiet, sleepy, just the way the locals liked it I guess. Dad called them hillbillies because they kept to themselves and didn't welcome nosy people looking for cheap properties to develop. They may have been isolated enough to see off the first wave of the virus but, like Angowrie, people fleeing the cities would have brought it eventually.

'Is there any way out of Megs to the north?' Kas asks.

'Bush tracks, for sure,' I say. 'But they'd be overgrown by now.'

'It sounds perfect,' Daymu says. 'We'd be protected from the north. We'd only have to keep watch on the road, and we could disappear into the bush if the decontamination teams came.'

We all look from one to another, each trying to work through the consequences of leaving Angowrie. My first thought is for Daymu. Her ankle is healing but she's still limping—and both she and JT could do with more time to recover from their journey. They'd need to be fitter if we have to run.

'Can we all agree on one thing?' JT says. 'We stick together. All of us.' He reaches into the middle of the table and places his hand flat on the surface. Daymu puts hers over his, then Kas adds hers and I lay mine on top. Only Ray holds back.

'Not me,' he says. 'I'm staying put. I'm too old to run. And if you had to take off into the bush, I couldn't keep up.' There's nothing bitter in his voice. He's been thinking about this for a while.

'But Ray—' I say.

'I don't want to run, Finn. I want to stay here. And what are they gonna do with me anyway? Pointless them taking me back to Longley. I don't have the virus. I don't need their medical services. I reckon I can talk them into letting me stay. I could be new unofficial mayor of Angowrie.'

This makes us laugh.

What he's saying makes some sense, but I hate the idea of leaving him on his own.

'It's okay, son,' he says, leaning over to place his hand on my shoulder. 'And besides, I can put them off the scent, tell them you headed towards Wentworth.'

It's only now that I see how tired Ray looks, like he's lost weight while the rest of us have been putting it on. He's moving slower too. He avoids sitting down because of the effort it takes to get back up. And this makes me worry about how he'll cope here on his own.

Kas walks behind him and puts her arms around his neck. Ray pats her hand and says, 'You'll be right, girl. Things'll work out.'

6

There's a new urgency about everything we do the next day as we get organised to leave. Part of our preparation involves setting Ray up in another house, away from the storage garage. When the decontamination squads find him, they'll want to know where he's been living and how he's survived. To keep prying eyes away from our stores we need to make another house looks like it's only been inhabited by Ray. We find a place at the top of Parker Street that's perfect, a brick house with all its windows intact and a roof that didn't blow off in the storms last winter. It'll make sense that a survivor would choose a place high up, where they could keep watch for trouble.

We've made saddlebags for the horses and each of us has a small pack. Kas and I try to convince Daymu she should ride, but she's having none of it. The cut on JT's head has only partially healed, but a scab has formed and his hair is starting to grow back. It's going to be a slow trip, made slower by the condition of the road. The weather seems to be getting hotter— if that's possible—so we agree to travel by night, resting up in the forest during the heat of the day. We reckon we can get to Megs in about two days if there are no hold ups.

In the afternoon, we take Ray up Parker Street to show him his new home. He likes it. 'Solid,' he says, patting the bricks by the front door. 'And I don't mind the million-dollar view, either.' From the verandah he can see right up the river to the shops and the road winding into town. He'll get plenty of warning when the decontamination squads arrive. And he's got views along the coast to the east, where Red Rocks juts out into the strait. He points to it, then traces the lie of land north. 'About there,' he says, fixing on a ridgeline. 'That's my place. Not that there's much left of it now. Wilders saw to that.'

We're leaving tonight. The saddlebags are packed and we've made sure Yogi and Bess have been well fed and watered. Rowdy knows something is up. He doesn't let me out of his sight all afternoon. We gather in the kitchen and double-check our packs. We want to take as much as we can but we also know we'll have to move quickly if there's trouble on the road. We spread the map on the table and pinpoint Devils Elbow, a corner where the road switches back inland, as our destination for the night. We can drop off the side of the road and climb down to a little creek mouth, maybe find a cave or overhang to sleep in during the day.

We've got a couple of hours until it gets dark so I take Kas up the river to the footbridge near the playground.

'Where are we going?' she asks.

'Home,' I say.

The old house has taken a battering from the storms, but it's still standing. Rowdy has followed us but he stops short of the driveway and waits. Most of the windows are broken and around the back a big branch has fallen across the shed. The roof buckles in the middle and the door has been pushed out by the impact. I can't bring myself to look inside. I know the memories it holds, in the smell of the place and the empty tool racks. I don't want to think of Dad working away, sanding some old piece of furniture or tinkering with the mower.

Kas is quiet but she's watching me. She follows me inside the house. I pause at the backdoor, remembering the day I came home and found Mum sick with the virus. She was slumped at the kitchen table, crying and telling me not to come near her. A shiver passes through me, and Kas's hands slip around my arm.

'You've never shown me any photos,' she says. 'Of your mum and dad.'

'I don't have any,' I say.

'None?' she asks.

'I burned them. All of them.'

'What? Why?'

I think about the day I gathered all the photos together, about a month after mum died. I couldn't bear to look at them. I thought about putting them away somewhere, so I'd still have them after the grief had eased, but I knew it would only make things harder.

'I guess it was my way of letting go,' I say, though that's only half true. I was angry at being left alone. In a way I blamed myself for surviving when Mum and Dad didn't. But I'd love to have the photos now, to show Kas and to keep with me. I can barely remember what Mum and Dad looked like.

Kas pulls me closer. She knows what loss does to people. Everyone reacts differently.

I'm not sure what I expect to feel in the house, but there's a hollowness inside me, like I've been away too long. Too much has happened since I left here, too many events have crowded in and pushed the memories aside.

There's one place I've been avoiding. The grass and creepers have taken over the garden but the mound is still visible. I may have forgotten a lot but the night we buried Dad is burned inside me somewhere deep. Mum and I took it in turns to dig, both of us wiping away the tears and striking the ground with our spades to let out the anger. We rolled Dad's body into a blue tarp but blood trickled out when we moved him. It took all our strength to lower him in without dropping him. I can still hear the sound of the dirt on the tarp, still see the blue slowly being covered with the black soil.

I kneel down and push some of the creepers back to see the stone we set on top of the grave. I found it on the beach, and we wrote on it in permanent marker.

Tom Morrison
Husband, father, top bloke
Rest in peace

Kas squats behind me. 'I wish I'd met him,' she says.

'He would've liked you,' I say, brushing the dirt off my hands. 'He was straight up. No bullshit. He said what he meant and it got him in trouble sometimes.'

'Ha,' she says, and I hear a little snort. 'I definitely would've liked him, then.'

Back at the house, we know we have to get going but it's still too hot to travel so we wait another hour for the heat to fall out of the day. Most evenings a cool breeze off the ocean wrestles with the northerly and eventually wins. We're in the kitchen again, knowing it's the last time we'll see Ray for a while. He's quiet, gazing at each of us in turn, like he's trying to memorise our faces. He catches me looking and winks. Rowdy sidles up to him and Ray scratches him behind the ears.

Kas squats on the floor, her back against the fridge. She asks Daymu if she's heard anything about her brother.

Daymu shakes her head and tears well in her eyes.

'I didn't know you had a brother,' Ray says, always the one trying to ease the tension from a situation.

Daymu seems happy for the distraction. 'Ashin and me, we came through the detention centre on Christmas Island. Our boat sank near Ashmore Reef and the border patrol picked us up.'

'And you were sold when you got here?' Ray asks.

Daymu takes a deep breath, her eyes fixed on the floor. 'Being brother and sister, they sold us as a pair,' she says, 'to a farmer called Heathcote. Out near Simpson, north of Longley.'

The way she says the farmer's name, curling her lip, gives me a sense of where the story is going.

'You know what they were like,' she says. 'He had no wife or kids. He beat us if he thought we weren't working hard enough. Ashin copped the worst of it, but we looked out for each other, made sure neither of us was ever alone with him.'

'Is your brother older than you?' I ask.

'Yeah, by two minutes,' she says, smiling.

'You're twins!'

'We look so much alike,' she says. 'If I cut my hair you wouldn't be able to tell us apart.' She looks up and her eyes wander towards the window. Her face glows when she talks about Ashin. 'I miss him so much,' she says.

'How were you separated?' Kas asks.

'Heathcote died from the virus. We survived for a while on our own but the Wilders were rounding up kids off the farms. I was caught in the open. I screamed and yelled to warn Ashin, and I haven't seen him since that morning.'

I can't help but feel guilty about all this having gone on—even before the virus—and me not knowing anything about it. Mum and Dad must have known. Did they protect me from it? Did they feel helpless in the face of the authorities that allowed it to happen?

It's getting noticeably cooler inside. The sun is dropping

behind the trees and a breeze pushes at the curtains. It's time. JT is the first to his feet and he pulls Daymu up by her hand.

Kas's mouth is set in a tight line as she looks at Ray. 'We'd better get the horses,' she says.

We sling the saddlebags across Yogi and Bess, and secure them with straps underneath. We've made a leather sleeve for the rifle and we tie it to Yogi's side. We're taking three rabbit traps. We bind them up with tape to stop them jangling with the swaying of the horses.

Kas is moving slow and deliberate, drawing out our leaving. It's like everything we know is coming to an end—our summer here with Ray, the surfing, the swimming and hunting, the routine of what was almost a normal life.

We lock up the house and put branches and rubbish up against the walls and door. We've already made the garage look as unused as we can.

'I'll walk out to the road with you,' Ray says. I reckon he's trying hard to sound matter-of-fact but his eyes tell a different story.

We cross Parker Street and make our way to the coast road.

'This is it for me,' Ray says. 'Bloody hard enough getting up the hill without going any further.' His smile seems to crease his whole face, his eyes disappearing into the deep lines of his cheeks. 'Don't make it any harder than it is,' he says, raising a hand in a wave. 'Just go.'

But Kas passes Yogi's reins to JT and she and I walk into Ray's arms. He takes Kas's face in his weathered hands and kisses the top of her head. He smells of wood smoke.

'Righto,' he says, holding us at arm's length. 'Enough of that; you'd better get going.'

'Look after yourself, Ray,' I say.

'Always do,' he replies. 'Now bugger off, you lot. I've gotta get some dinner organised.' He gives Rowdy a last scratch behind the ears. 'Look after them, boy,' he says. 'And try not to get shot this time.'

Heat lingers in the air but the sea breeze cools us as we climb the hill beyond the lookout platform. From up here the road stretches out like a ribbon along the coast. Only the reassuring sound of Yogi and Bess's hoofs rises above the roar of the ocean.

There's less storm debris here than further north, but in places the dunes have completely reclaimed the bitumen. The tide's too high for the beach to be an alternative so we're forced to trudge through the heavy, dry sand that covers the road.

The night closes in on us. I keep an eye on Daymu and JT. They seem to be moving okay but they're slower than Kas and me. Every now and again I feel Rowdy push past my leg. The stars appear one by one, and before long the whole Milky Way has spread itself across the sky. A sliver of moon rises behind us.

It's hard leaving Angowrie. These last few months it's been a sanctuary. Our familiarity with it—the rhythm of the tide in and out of the river mouth, the salty smell of the under-growth, the humidity after rain—they've all fed into a sense of belonging we've taken for granted. Out here on the road I feel exposed, less sure of where to run, where to hide, how to outmanoeuvre an enemy.

It's a long night. Kas and I have stayed fit through hunting, swimming and surfing, but walking this sort of distance is different. Apart from the shifting dunes, we have to negotiate a few fallen trees but they're only small stringbarks and scrubby melaleucas, and we get around them pretty easily. By the time the sky begins to lighten in the east, we're within reach of Devils Elbow, the last place we can access the beach before the road disappears into the forest.

JT and Daymu have fallen behind so we wait for them catch up. They're exhausted. We drop off into an old car park with picnic tables set under some tea trees. We don't want to risk a fire so we eat a rabbit Ray cooked up yesterday. It's the only meat we brought with us and we know it won't keep in the heat. From here on we'll have to rely on what we can hunt with the rifle, though we're reluctant to use the bullets in case we need them to protect ourselves.

When the sun is fully up we pull the horses into a clump of moonah where they can't be seen from the road. We find a cool spot under a rock overhang to lay out the sleeping bags. It's too hot to get inside them but they give a bit of cushioning on the hard ground. Daymu volunteers to take the first sentry duty. Kas and I try to convince her she should sleep but she ignores us and climbs up to find a spot with a view of the road. I'm tired but my brain is buzzing with anticipation of what lies ahead tonight. It'll be the most dangerous part of the journey. There's a scenic lookout marked on the map at the tip of Cape Petrel. Once we get past there the road descends another ten k's to Megs Creek.

I feel like I've hardly slept when JT nudges me with his foot and hands me the rifle for my turn at sentry duty. It's mid-afternoon and the sun is blazing. I find a tree clinging to the steep ground and lean my back against the trunk. Way off in the distance, the point by the rock pools sticks out into the blue haze of the ocean and beyond that I can just make out the granite boulders of Red Rocks.

It's a relief when the sun finally starts to drop. The ridges give us shade a couple of hours before sunset.

Kas climbs up towards me, moving fast.

I'm on my feet, worried, scanning the road. 'What is it?' I ask.

She rubs the lump on the back of her hand where the tracking device sits under her skin. 'I felt it vibrate,' she says. 'Just now.'

I put my hand over hers and we wait.

Nothing.

'Are you sure?' I ask.

'Definitely. What if it's live, Finn? What if they know where we are?'

'I dunno,' I say, holding her hand tighter. 'But we need to get started if we're going to make Megs Creek tonight.' We help each other down, moving as quickly as we dare on the steep ground.

JT and Daymu are on the beach. Daymu stands in the shallows in her shorts and splashes water onto her face and arms. JT has stripped off and dived in.

Kas runs to Daymu and I see them touch each other's tracker. Daymu nods.

With twilight taking hold, we load the horses and move

out to the road. We've told JT about the trackers, and there's urgency in everything we do. I can't help looking behind us towards Angowrie, peering into the gloom for any sign of movement. I have a gnawing sense of something being very wrong. We're exposed here—and we're in a worse situation than we would've been if we'd stayed at home. At least there we knew where to hide.

The road begins its steady climb into the forest. There are half a dozen hairpin bends where the trees lean in over the top of us. It's eerie being so enclosed after the openness of the coast. We are out of the wind and every footfall of the horses is exaggerated by the stillness. We keep a steady pace until the bitumen winds back towards the clifftops. The trees give way to sheer walls of rock on the inland side and only the metal barrier separates us from the drop into the ocean on our left. According to the map, there's five kilometres of this leading up to Cape Petrel. JT slides the rifle out of its sleeve and hangs it over his shoulder.

'All together, or spread out?' he asks.

'Stay as we are, I reckon,' Kas says. 'But be ready to run.'

The night drags. We walk as fast as we can but it takes forever to get to the cape. Eventually though, the roadside lookout comes into view. We round a corner and see it a couple of hundred metres ahead. I begin to breathe a little easier. JT throws me a smile and a quick nod. We're almost there. At the tip of the cape there's a small car park edged by a stone wall. The sea is so far below us we can't hear it and the wind pushes up the cliff faces and across the road. We reach the car park and decide to take a quick rest, sitting with our backs to the wall and stretching our legs.

It's well past midnight. The moon and stars are hidden behind cloud.

'No time for slacking off,' I say.

Kas and Daymu take their turn leading the horses, while JT and I follow behind.

Leaving the lookout we round a tight corner before starting the descent. Daymu and Kas are ahead of us as we get to the bend.

Suddenly, the road is flooded with light.

7

The horses shy and skitter on the asphalt. We're totally blinded but our first instinct is to turn and run. Then I hear the revving of a truck engine coming up behind us.

Men are shouting. 'Get down! Get down on the ground. Drop the rifle.'

I pull Kas towards me and lie next to her. JT and Daymu are beside us. The road is covered with loose stones and they dig into my bare legs. I grab Rowdy by the collar. He's growling and I put a hand over his mouth to keep him quiet.

I look up, shielding my eyes, but I can't make anyone out. The truck behind us has come to a halt. The engine rumbles and whines and finally switches off, letting out a slow wheeze as everything falls silent.

Boots edge towards us, and a knee drops onto my back, forcing my face into the road. Cable ties loop my wrists and are pulled tight. Eventually, the four of us are dragged to our feet and made to stand in a line in front of the first truck. Rowdy stays by my side and I can vaguely make out Yogi and Bess. Someone's got their reins.

A stooped, thick figure is silhouetted in the glare. I don't have to hear his voice to know it's Tusker.

'I told you,' he says, triumphant. 'I told you I'd find you, didn't I.'

He comes up close to Kas and sniffs. 'I thought you said you'd smell me coming?' he says. 'Well smell this.' He grabs her by the hair and pulls her face to his chest and down to his crotch. Kas writhes, trying to head butt him but Tusker laughs.

I lurch towards him but something heavy hits me across the head and I stumble sideways. I realise then I'm tied to JT, and he falls on top of me. I try to steady myself on the ground, but a boot comes out of the glare and kicks my arms from underneath me. My head slams into JT's and the salty taste of blood fills my mouth.

Kas has somehow got to her feet. She takes a few paces back from Tusker then launches herself, barreling into him. He staggers with the impact and loses his footing. She kicks wildly at him before she's pulled away and thrown to the ground.

When Tusker sits up he's laughing again. 'See, boys,' he yells. 'She can't resist me!'

He stands up and does a little jig, dancing from one foot to the other, then turns and faces the lights, his arms spread like a preacher. 'What a great night this is,' he says, his voice rising. 'Revenge!' he howls. 'Revenge against the Sileys who brought the virus—and against the bastards who protected them.'

Every sentence is met with cheers. I can't tell how many men there are but it sounds like a lot.

'This is the new world,' he continues, his voice lower now. 'We're in charge and we'll decide who comes into our country.'

More cheers.

Finally, he draws breath. 'Kill those lights,' he barks over his shoulder, and we're plunged into darkness.

Slowly our eyes adapt to the dark, and the hulking shapes of the trucks emerge. Both of them have bulldozer blades on the front. Tusker looks smaller without the glare of the lights but I can now see about a dozen men encircling us. Two of them pull Daymu to her feet, while Tusker drags Kas up by her hair. Her breath comes in short bursts. He pulls her head back so she has to look him in the face. He traces her birthmark with his fingertip and slides his other hand down the front of her T-shirt. Kas turns away but he jerks her back and tries to kiss her. I blindly throw myself at her, pulling JT with me, but Tusker steps in front of us.

'Hello, hero boy,' he snarls. 'We meet again.' He brings his face close enough that I can smell his acid breath. Then he leans into me and whispers, 'She's mine now. I'll collect the bounty, but until I do...'

Another man grabs me from behind. He shoves JT so my

arms are wrenched sideways then grabs my ears to hold me still. Tusker pulls me over to Kas. A crooked smile twists his face. He takes a knife from his belt and sticks the point of it under my chin.

'This remind you of anything?' he asks Kas.

'Don't,' she cries. 'I cut you. It wasn't him.'

'Nice try, girl,' Tusker says, 'but we can't have you damaged.' He turns the knife so the blade is against my skin. I rise onto my toes, lifting my chin, but the knife follows. As he leers at Kas, Tusker slowly increases the pressure until I feel the edge begin to cut. I'm staring ahead, trying not to cry out. Blood trickles down my neck and inside my shirt.

'I'm sorry, Finn,' Kas whispers. 'I'm sorry.'

'Enough fun for now,' Tusker yells. 'Huddo, put the Sileys in our truck. Gordon, the other two in yours. We've got a long night ahead.'

JT and I are pulled towards the back of one of the trucks. We try to hold our ground but sharp blows to our legs keep us moving forward. Blood is dripping off my chin.

I call out to Kas.

'*Finnnnnn*,' she screams before she and Daymu are dragged into the other truck.

We're lifted onto the tray and thrown forward onto the metal floor. Rowdy leaps up and cringes in the far corner. Only one of the men climbs in after us. He sits opposite us, cradling a rifle. The truck lurches backwards and swings forwards as the driver turns it towards Lewtas Bay. The other truck passes us and we follow.

A few minutes pass before JT and I manage to push ourselves up so we're sitting back to back. I bring my chin to my shoulder to try to feel the depth of the cut. There's blood on the floor where I was lying.

A canvas canopy encloses the truck. It beats against the metal supports as we pick up speed. JT and I try to brace with our feet each time we turn a corner or swerve to avoid debris but we slide helplessly from side to side.

I replay the night over and over in my mind, trying to think of what we could have done to avoid this. But every idea ends up being drowned out by the memory of Kas screaming my name. My muscles tense when I think of the way Tusker pawed at her and pushed her head into his crotch.

I promise myself I'll find her. I won't give up until she's safe. And Tusker is dead.

Rowdy has edged out from under the seat where he's been hiding. The Wilder doesn't show any interest in him.

Eventually, we reach a straighter section of road and it's easier to hold ourselves still. The back flap is open and the night air rushes in. The clouds have cleared and there's enough moon to see by. I try to focus on our guard. He looks familiar—youngish, with a round face and thin beard. He wears a glove on one hand.

'Didn't think I'd be seeing you again,' he says.

I've heard that voice before.

'Col,' he says, finally.

It's the Wilder who was guarding Sylvia and Hope at the Ramsay farm. He pulls a rag out of his pocket, puts it over my chin and knots it on top of my head. 'That's a mess,' he says. 'You're lucky he didn't slit your throat.'

'Reckon we're probably worth more alive than dead,' I say. My voice sounds even stranger than normal with the rag forcing me to mumble.

Col looks at me like he's weighing up whether to tell me something. 'Maybe. But they only pay bounties on Sileys.'

'They?'

'The authorities in Wentworth' he says, his voice rising above the drone of the engine. 'That's where the girls'll be going.'

'When? How soon?'

Col shakes his head. 'Don't do it to yourself,' he says. 'They're gone. You'll never see them again.'

It's not so much what he says but the way he says it—with total indifference—that worries me.

'And us?' I ask. I feel JT pushing against me, letting me know he's listening.

'There's no sympathy for anyone hiding Sileys,' he says.

'What will happen?' I ask.

'It varies. They brought a bloke in last month, been shacked up with a Siley girl. He disappeared one night and the girl was sent to Wentworth.'

'To be sold, you mean,' I say.

'They're Sileys,' he says, his voice harder.

'Sylvia was a Siley,' I say.

Col seems shocked that I remember her name. He sits back and his face disappears into the shadows for a few seconds.

'What happened to her?' I ask.

'We tried to run,' he says, leaning forward again. He grinds his jaw as though he's trying to stop the words coming out. 'They tracked us. Took them a week, but they found us.'

'Sylvia?' I ask.

'Taken to Wentworth,' he says.

'And you—?'

He doesn't say anything but carefully pulls the glove off his hand. Two of his fingers are missing. There are black scabs at the knuckles.

'Ramage did that?' I ask.

He shakes his head. 'Tusker,' he says. 'It's hard to believe, but he's worse.'

'What about the army?' I say.

'All based in Wentworth. They're not too worried how the zones are controlled, as long as the Sileys are hunted down and brought back.'

'But—' I'm trying to figure out how much power Ramage wields. 'What's happening in Wentworth?'

'I haven't been there,' he says. 'But I've heard they're getting back on their feet—growing food, factories starting up again, shops opening.' He pulls the glove back onto his hand.

'What about the detention centre at Longley?' I ask, trying to keep him talking. 'Is that where we're headed now?'

He takes his time to answer. I get the impression he's already told us more than he thinks he should have. 'They'll take you two there—probably go through the motions of a trial.'

'A trial?'

'Ramage is the regional commissioner. That makes him

judge and jury,' he says. 'Tusker's the executioner.'

'Did you have a trial?' I ask Col.

'That's what they called it.'

'And your hand. That was the punishment?'

He nods. 'They need men to go on patrols, maintain their power,' he says. 'So they don't kill us.'

Things have gone to shit tonight but my brain is firing, trying to gather as much information as I can. I have to find a way to get to Kas. 'What's happened with the No-landers?' I ask.

A smile creases Col's lips. 'No-landers,' he says. 'Is that what you call them?'

'That's what they call themselves,' JT says, leaning up against me and shuffling around so he's looking at Col side on.

'They've caused havoc all summer. They keep moving. They attacked two farms in two days. Thirty kilometres apart! Christ knows how they move so fast on foot.'

I've seen how fast Tahir and Gabriel walk. I reckon thirty k's would be a short stroll for them. 'Tell us about the detention centre,' I say.

'The army set it up, left half a dozen soldiers there. A doctor comes and goes. They keep themselves separate from the rest of us— hardly come into town unless there's a trial.'

'And what about Ramage?' I ask.

'He still uses the feedstore as his base,' he says. 'He doesn't let the authorities know half of what he's doing. Even then, the soldiers don't care, most of them. They hate being out in the zone.'

The mention of the feedstore sends a shiver through me. I

can't bear to think of Kas being held there again. My skin crawls with the thought of what Tusker and Ramage could do to her.

Col must see the look on my face.

'Sileys are the property of the bounty hunters until payment's made,' he says. 'They'll go straight to the feedstore, then to Wentworth within a couple of days.'

Col sounds defeated, different from the cocky bloke we met last spring. I wonder if this is what happens to everybody under Ramage—they give up and do whatever he says.

I try for more information. 'You know the valley farm?' I ask. 'Where the trouble was last year?'

'What about it?' Col says.

'What's happened to them? The farmers.'

'I dunno. I haven't heard. Not that I would—Ramage and Tusker don't tell us anything. They're inside the Longley zone, though, so—'

'And the baby, Hope. Did you see her again?'

'No. There's no baby in Longley. I would've heard about that.'

I'm exhausted from the long night of walking and bruised from the hits we copped when we were caught. Thankfully, the bleeding has stopped. JT and I roll to one side and lie down. At least we can stretch our legs this way. Rowdy pushes his nose into my face and licks at my chin. I doze on and off.

Eventually daylight creeps into the back of the truck. It feels like we're climbing again—the engine is labouring through the gears.

Col gives me a nudge with his foot. 'Not long now,' he says.

'We're almost over the range.'

JT and I struggle to a sitting position. Out the back of the canopy the forest is deep green and grey in the morning light. The truck gains speed and we lurch around corners as we descend. The trees give way to rolling farmland, all of it deserted.

'It took them most of the summer to clear this road,' Col says. 'It'll all be colonised out here soon.'

'Who by?' I say.

A smile crosses his lips. 'They need experienced farmers,' he says.

'So that's why you've given up. Why you're part of this.'

There's coldness in his stare. 'Can I give you some advice? Don't fight it—you'll only lose. You might not like it but the world's not going to change anytime soon. There aren't enough people left to fight the good fight. You've gotta adapt.'

I feel like I've heard this so many times over the last year. A niggling thought in the back of my mind tells me it might be right. All I've succeeded in doing is making powerful enemies. I'm captured and separated from Kas, and our lives mean nothing to these people.

The sun is streaming in by the time we reach the highway. It's warm under the canvas and the metal tray is heating up, too. There are no other vehicles on the road, but every so often we swerve to avoid some obstacle. Gateways lead to abandoned farms, their driveways lined by hedges grown wild. But as we get closer to Longley, we pass paddocks with a few cows and sheep grazing on what's left of the dry grass, and armed

66

guards keeping watch. When we reach the outskirts of town, we pass smaller properties with their houses close to the road. They look like working farms. The truck slows and we turn off, winding our way along a dirt track, the dust lifting and choking us. When we come to a stop, two soldiers in uniform look over the tailgate and check us out.

'Two?' one of them says to Col.

'Yep,' he replies.

I hear a banging on the side of the truck. We move forward and high wire gates close behind us. The tailgate drops with a loud clang and Col lifts JT and me to our feet. He steadies us so we can ease down to the ground.

'Good luck, boys,' he says, before walking back in the direction of the gates. 'And watch out for the dog. They won't like it.'

8

The sunlight is blinding. There's no sign of the other truck with Kas and Daymu. The compound is made up of a large shed and half a dozen brick houses, all low-slung with wide verandahs. Two long buildings that look like dormitories have bars on the windows and guards at the doors.

Rowdy sniffs everything, peeing against posts and fences. Otherwise, he stays close.

With a soldier behind, prodding us with his rifle, we shuffle towards the big corrugated-iron shed next to one of the dormitories. It looks like a machinery workshop. Out the front, a lone petrol bowser sits in the sun, a chain pulled tight through the nozzle and padlocked to the side. In the shed, there are block-and-tackle hoists hanging from a steel gantry and four pits in the concrete floor for working under vehicles. JT and I are pushed towards the steps that drop into one of the pits. We have to edge our way down sideways to stop from falling.

Our guard seems to notice Rowdy for the first time. 'What's this, then?' he says. 'A boy's best friend?' He coaxes Rowdy towards him before grabbing him by the scruff of the neck. Rowdy wheels around and tries to bite him, but the soldier is too quick. He slides a length of rope through Rowdy's collar and drags him to the wall to tie him up.

The shed's iron roof and walls magnify the heat, and the floor of the pit is greasy with oil. Sweat is streaming off me, and it feels like the wound on my chin has opened up again. JT and I lean against each other and wait. The guard has pulled a chair over and he sits on the lip of the pit, his rifle resting in his lap. He seems bored, constantly checking the doorway as though he's expecting someone.

'How long are you going to keep us here?' JT asks, but the guard ignores us. 'What about some water?' JT tries again.

This time JT gets his attention. He pulls a drink flask off his belt, unscrews the lid slowly and takes a long drink. He gives an exaggerated, 'Ahhh...' when he's finished, even allowing a little trickle to run down his chin and drip onto his shirt.

When we turn away he becomes agitated, leaning forward in his chair. 'You're collaborators,' he says. 'Do you have any idea the damage Sileys are doing? They brought the virus in the first place and now they're trying to take over.' He pauses for effect, pointing at us. 'And you,' he says. 'What do you do? You hide them from us. Where's your loyalty? You're both patriots aren't you?'

Patriots. It's a word I heard on the news when they first started bringing Sileys from offshore. There were big rallies— protesters with their faces covered by balaclavas, holding flags and chanting anti-Siley slogans. They faced off against the other side, the pro-Siley groups objecting to the slave auctions. 'Patriots!' Dad had said, turning the TV off. 'More like thugs and dickheads.'

'Have you ever met a Siley?' JT asks. 'They're no different from us.'

The soldier laughs. 'You've been brainwashed by the bleed- ing-hearts. No wonder the country's on its knees. We're trying to rebuild something here, but idiots like you are undermining us at every turn. You deserve everything that's coming to you.'

I try to ignore him but his words sting. Kas and Daymu are gone, we're at the mercy of Ramage and there's no way of pleading our case.

Sometime around midday, there's movement in the yard and the sound of voices. Steps echo across the concrete floor, and our guard gets to his feet. Three people appear above us, two men and a woman. The woman doesn't wear a uniform and she has a band around her arm with a red cross on it. A mask covers her nose and mouth. She descends into the pit, looks at my eyes and puts her hand to my forehead.

'How long have they been here?' she asks. There's nothing in her voice to tell me her standing with the soldiers.

'Not long,' the guard answers.

'All morning,' JT says, his mouth so dry his voice is barely a whisper.

The woman turns and climbs out of the pit. 'Bring them to the infirmary,' she says, as she leaves.

The two soldiers who came with her step down and lift us to our feet.

'Take your time,' our guard spits. 'Make her wait.'

Rowdy strains at his rope, barking and fretting. 'I'll be back soon,' I call to him, not knowing whether it's true or not.

Our boots are coated with oil and grease so our feet keep sliding out from under us as we're pulled into the hot morning. Each time we slip, the cable ties cut further into our wrists. The sun hits us like a sledgehammer. We are taken to one of the brick buildings. There are vines growing up a trellis onto the roof. Inside, it's cool and dark. Along a wide corridor, open doors lead to rooms with empty beds with clean sheets and pillows.

In the last room, the woman sits, drumming her fingers on the desk. She tells the guards to wait outside, shuts the door and pulls a pair of scissors from her pocket to cut the cable ties. JT and I have hardly got the strength to move, but we shake our arms and flex our wrists, trying to get the blood flowing to our hands again.

'Bastards,' the woman says, loud enough for us to hear, but not the guards outside. She fills two glasses with water and hands them to us. I pull the handkerchief away from my chin. It's dry and it tears at the wound. We drink quickly and she refills the glasses.

She shines a small torch into our eyes, double checks, then removes the mask from her face.

Her skin is light brown, her eyes dark and her black hair is cut short but neat. We're reluctant to sit down because our clothes are filthy, but she insists. She squats in front of us. 'Where did they capture you?' she asks.

JT gives me a sideways glance and shakes his head.

'On the coast,' I say, warily.

She raises her eyebrows. 'The coast? I didn't know there was anyone left alive down there.'

I shrug. The way she acts towards the guards makes me want to trust her but I'm wary—why would she be here if she wasn't working with the army?

On the back of her left hand I spy a familiar lump. She stands up and leans on the desk, touching the tracking device under her skin. 'Yeah, I'm a Siley,' she says.

'But you're...'

'A doctor? Yes. I get sent out to the zones to check on any survivors brought in. Make sure they're not virus carriers.'

I find myself warming to her, wanting to trust her. She doesn't seem to be holding anything back from us. 'Where are you from? Originally, I mean?' I ask.

'Originally?' she says. 'I was born here. But my parents came years ago—so I got reclassified when the virus hit. They don't care anymore. It's difference they're scared of—anyone with dark skin, a different religion, a strange language.'

I change tack, trying for more information. 'So,' I ask, 'are the tracking devices working again?'

She takes her time to answer.

'No one knows for sure, but there are more Sileys being caught every day.'

There's a sharp rap on the door and a male voice, 'Hurry up.'

She slips on a pair of latex gloves and starts to check us over. She takes our temperature and blood pressure. 'That cut needs stitches,' she says, gently lifting my head to examine the gash. 'It's going to hurt. I don't have any anesthetic, sorry.'

She pulls out two syringes and apologises again. 'I have to take blood samples. Check for the virus.'

JT cuts in. 'Who are you?' he asks.

She smiles, showing even white teeth. 'I'm Angela,' she says.

I need to take a chance. She's been open with us, as best we can tell. Maybe she knows about the feedstore. 'When we were captured,' I say. 'There were four of us. Me, JT, Kas and Daymu.'

'Girls?'

'Yeah. Sileys. And Ramage has them.'

'I'm sorry,' she says, writing their names down on a pad on her desk.

As we roll up our sleeves I whisper, 'What's happening in the cities?'

She tightens a strap around my bicep and speaks low and fast as she works. 'Wentworth is recovering,' she says. 'The army's in control but they need Sileys to do a lot of the work. They're tolerating Ramage for now, but I can't see him lasting. They've made him a commissioner, but he's just a criminal.'

I'm tempted to tell her everything that's happened with Ramage over the past year, but we don't have time. 'Yeah, we've met him,' is all I say.

'And you're alive,' she says. 'You've done better than most.' Her fingers trace the brand on my forearm. 'Not unscathed, though.'

She draws blood into the syringe and eases the needle from my arm, before moving on to JT. She works quickly and efficiently and in a minute she has a vial from both of us.

'What about the virus?' I ask.

She doesn't hesitate. The more she speaks the more I think she's on our side. 'It's still active and it mutates fast. As soon as they think they've isolated it, a different strain crops up somewhere else. The only thing they know for sure is that it's airborne.'

'Airborne?'

She sighs. 'It's almost impossible to contain. And, the symptoms are changing.'

'How?'

'There's a new strain. It shows in the eyes first—the irises turn yellow and the lids get crusty.'

'We haven't seen anything like that.'

'If you do, run.'

'And what about the rest of the country?'

'Communications are still very basic. We just don't know, but I've heard towns are turning into fortresses—fenced and guarded. And the weather is crazy—cyclones further south, drought, bushfires in winter. So much infrastructure destroyed.'

She opens a sealed packet with swabs and a curved needle. 'I'll be as gentle as I can,' she says. 'Try not to move.'

She takes the needle, pinches the skin under my chin and draws the thread through. I grip the arms of my chair and try not to shake too much. I distract myself by thinking of Rose, sitting at my kitchen table and sewing her own hand. Tears well in my eyes and Angela wipes them away with a piece of gauze. 'Nearly done,' she says.

'Is there anything else you can tell us?' JT asks, his voice low and urgent.

'If you escape,' she says, 'stay away from Wentworth. Head back to the coast. Forget the girls.'

She gives the thread a final tug and ties it off.

'You'll have a scar to show for it,' she says. 'But it'll heal as long as you keep it clean.' She pushes a couple of packets of sterile swabs into my hand. 'Keep these out of sight,' she says.

There's knocking at the door again and this time the guard steps into the room. Angela leans into us. 'Stay safe,' she says.

'You too,' I say.

'Come on,' the guard says, louder than necessary. 'Get a move on.' He grabs us by the back of our shirts and pulls us to our feet. He notes the cable ties on the floor and glares at Angela, who does her best to ignore him.

'One more thing,' I say before we're bundled out of the room. 'Rowdy, my dog. He's tied up in the shed.'

'No promises,' she says, 'but I'll see what I can do.'

Outside we are led to one of the dormitories with bars on the windows. Inside it's hot and stuffy. We're hustled into the first cell before we can see if there are any other prisoners here. The door is shut and we hear a bolt slide into place. The floor is concrete and the only window, high in the back wall, allows the wind to heat the room even more. We sit against the wall and stretch our legs out in front of us.

'What do you make of the doc?' JT asks.

'She seems pretty genuine,' I say.

'What she said about Wentworth—'

'Yeah, I know. But if that's where they're sending Kas and Daymu—'

'We have to get there, somehow.'

'Agreed.'

When I start to cramp, I ease myself onto the floor and JT does the same. It's cooler down low but the concrete digs into my hips. My chin feels tights and sore. I touch it with my thumb, feeling the little prickles of each stitch.

'Closest you'll come to growing a beard,' JT says. I don't turn to look at him but I can tell he's smiling.

'Smartarse,' I say.

Sometime later in the day, the door opens and a tray of food is pushed along the floor. There's only one bowl of thin soup, but there's a plastic bottle of water next to it. We take a swig each, being careful not to lose a drop.

The night, when it comes, is long and uncomfortable. The temperature drops away and we huddle together for warmth. It's a shitty situation but I'm grateful not to be on my own. A couple of times during the night I wake to the sound of a dog barking. It comes from a long way off and I can't tell if it's Rowdy.

When I do manage to sleep, it's from pure exhaustion. I dream of Kas, her face close to mine, her mouth open like she's screaming but no sound comes out. I reach for her but her body dissolves at my touch.

Deep in the night, we're woken by torches flashing in our faces. Strong hands lift me and I'm dragged through the door and across the corridor to another room.

A large figure sits at a desk, waiting. He stands up, strikes a match and lights a lamp hanging from the ceiling.

It's Ramage.

9

Ramage looks much older than he did last spring. His beard has been roughly clipped. His hair is cropped short and it's streaked with grey. The scar where I cut him rises in a ridge across the back of his hand.

'Sit down,' he says. He sounds tired, unwell.

He takes a pouch of tobacco from his shirt pocket and makes a point of rolling a cigarette slowly and deliberately, looking at me the whole time. He strikes another match, lights the cigarette and tilts his head to blow smoke into the air above us. He coughs and his chest rattles.

He leans back in his chair and waves the guards to leave.

Each drag of the cigarette sets off a coughing fit. He brings up phlegm and spits it into a rubbish bin.

'So, here we are again, Finn,' he says, smoke wafting around his face. 'The boot's on the other foot this time, though, isn't it. You had your chance, and now'—he lifts both his hands, palms up—'now it comes to this.'

In my head, I'm scrambling for ideas, trying to figure a way of helping Kas. 'We were no threat to you, down on the coast,' I say.

'You were a threat to everyone. What did you expect—that we'd leave you there? Pretend you hadn't broken the law? Killed people?'

I shouldn't antagonise him but I can't help myself. 'You're the expert at killing people,' I say.

Ramage draws a few more puffs from the cigarette before he stubs it, half smoked, in an ashtray on the desk. His fingers are stained yellow and his nails are long and chipped. 'Let's start this conversation again,' he says, scratching the stubble on his chin. 'You and your friend are both strong, fit young men. You know the country. The way I look at it, it'd be a waste to send you to Wentworth to spend the rest of your days working in some rat-infested factory or on the killing floor of an abattoir.'

He waits, giving me time to work out where he's heading. I can see him baiting his hook, preparing to lure me in.

'It doesn't have to be that way,' he says, finally. 'There's an alternative.'

'And what's that?' I say.

'You're a smart boy. I'm sure you can guess.'

'Stay here and be your slave instead?' I say.

'No,' he says. 'No, no, no—not a slave.' His voice has changed, like he's letting me in on some secret. He winks. 'We rule this part of the country. The army is only interested in Wentworth. All they want from us is a food supply. We provide it and they leave us alone.'

He takes the rollies from his pocket again and nudges the packet across the desk. 'Smoke?' he says.

I ignore it. 'You want us to join you?' I ask.

He nods—and a smile creeps across his lips again. 'We need new blood. The world's changed, Finn. And...' He pauses, as if deciding how much to tell me. 'I'm not well.' He lifts his eyebrows. 'I need lieutenants who know the country.'

'You seem to have enough of those already,' I say.

'True, but not many with your skills. I could use you and your friend. And I can make your life so much easier.'

'What about Kas and Daymu?' I ask.

'The Sileys?' Ramage sighs, his eyes wandering around the room. 'I can't help you there. I get cattle and seed for them.'

He focuses his attention back on me.

'Forget about them,' he says, his voice softening again. 'I know it's hard, but you have to move on. Adapt. I'm offering you a new start. Land, livestock, a place of your own if you want it.'

'In exchange for what?' I ask.

'Your loyalty.'

'Become Wilders, you mean?'

'We don't call ourselves that—never did.'

'So, what do you call yourselves?'

'Settlers.'

'I prefer Wilders,' I say.

The longer the conversation goes, the more Ramage thinks he's winning me over. He lays his hands flat on the desk, eyeballing me. 'I'm the commissioner, Finn. I can make this happen. Trust me.'

I'm reminded of the last time I spoke with Ramage in the valley—the way he twists things until they almost sound reasonable, so confident his offer is irresistible. He stands now, looking like he's going to reach out and shake my hand.

'Oh, there's one more thing,' he says, almost laughing. 'Guard!'

The door opens and a soldier appears holding Rowdy by the collar. As soon as he sees me, Rowdy frets and strains, his paws slipping on the lino floor.

I try to get out of my chair, to touch him, but Ramage's hands are on my shoulders, his mouth close to my ear. 'He hasn't stopped whining since you were dragged away.' He pauses, increasing the pressure on my shoulders. 'Join us and you can keep him. But if you reject my offer, well, the dog's just another mouth to feed.'

All I want is to hold Rowdy, to pat him and tell him he'll be okay. Ramage is digging his fingernails into my skin now. A howl comes from deep inside, so dark with hate and fear I can hardly believe it's me. 'No!' I yell. My voice is high and broken and spit flies out of my mouth.

'Last chance,' Ramage whispers.

Rowdy and I strain towards each other and I get close enough for him to lick my face.

'I'm sorry, boy,' I say. 'I'm sorry.'

Ramage hauls me back around to face him. 'I won't ask again,' he says, his voice thick with phlegm. 'Will you join us?'

'Never!' I say, but I can't look at Rowdy.

Ramage doesn't seem surprised. He lets go of me, folds his arms and sits against the desk. He turns to the guard. 'Kill the dog,' he says.

Rowdy is dragged out of the room, barking frantically now, and the door is closed. My face is in my hands and I'm howling. 'You bastard! You bastard.'

'Such a pity,' Ramage says. 'We could have made a good team, you and I. Like father and son.'

Another guard appears and I'm pulled, kicking and screaming, back to the cell.

We're both awake, sitting against the wall as the room starts to heat up with the new day. JT didn't say anything when I came back last night. I figure he overheard most of what happened anyway. He reached for me in the dark and put his arm around my shoulder.

'We really cocked this up, didn't we.' he says.

'We had to try. We couldn't just sit it out in Angowrie and hope for the best.' I run my finger across the stitches again and pull a swab out of my pocket to dab at them.

We're interrupted by the sound of the bolt sliding open. Three soldiers muscle their way in.

'Get up,' one says. He kicks me hard in the ankle.

'Where are we going?' JT asks.

'You'll see,' the soldier answers.

Cable ties are pulled tight around our wrists again, and we're led into the yard. I squint, trying to adjust to the glare, and look around for any sign of Rowdy.

'What happened to my dog?' I ask the nearest guard.

He smirks. 'How would I know, kid? Probably shot.'

A truck rolls across the yard and we're bundled into the back, this time with two armed soldiers. One is tall and lanky with a horsey sort of face and a crew cut, while the other is heavily built: short and tanned and muscles pushing against his shirt. He plays with his weapon, an automatic machine gun, flipping a catch on top over and over.

'Come on, hero,' the short one says, looking directly at me. 'Give me an excuse to shoot a collaborator.' He spits at my feet.

Dust finds its way through gaps in the canvas canopy as we pass through the gates and pick up speed. Within ten minutes we come to a halt and the flap is thrown open. We're in Longley. The main street stretches out, running downhill towards the railway line. The feedstore is on the right, only fifty metres away. There are two sentries at the gate, neither in uniform.

We're directed towards a yellow brick building. It's a court-house. My gut tightens—a horrible, clawing feeling like I'm going to be sick.

We sit on a bench in the foyer. Our guards stand either side, more formal now, like they're being watched, too. After a few minutes we hear footsteps coming through the door, and muffled voices. Kas comes first, a Wilder on either side, her feet dragging on the floor. Her hands are bound behind her and there's thick grey tape across her mouth. Blood trickles from a cut on her cheek.

'Kas!' I yell, before a punch to my stomach doubles me over. She turns and looks, her eyes wide. She tries to say something but the tape makes it impossible to understand.

Next comes Daymu and she looks worse than Kas. Her mouth is taped as well but her eyes are glazed, like she's barely conscious. JT leaps up but the stocky guard pulls him back down.

Kas and Daymu disappear inside the courtroom, and JT and I are left straining to follow them.

'Nice looking girlfriends they've got, Jackson,' the tall soldier says, smiling. 'Bet they'd be all right, eh? If they weren't Sileys.'

JT's eyes lock on the lanky guard. 'They're too good for a piece of shit like you,' he says.

Sometimes I wish JT wasn't such a bigmouth. He doesn't know when to shut up. The soldier curls his lip and looks like he's ready to lay into JT, but the one called Jackson shakes his head and says, 'Don't get sucked in, Murphy. These two'll cop it soon enough.'

Just then the doors open and we are taken inside. The courtroom is all wood panelling, with floor to ceiling windows on each side. Most of the seats are gone, but at the front there are half a dozen chairs facing the judge's bench. Kas and Daymu are propped against the wall. The Wilders stand next to them.

Sunlight streams through the windows, highlighting the dust

hanging in the air and turning it red and green.

We are pushed into the chairs. I can't take my eyes off Kas. She seems calmer now.

You okay? I mouth to her.

She blinks and nods her head.

A door behind the judge's table opens and two more Wilders file through. They look like all the others we've met in the last couple of years—bearded with long, matted hair and wearing clothes that don't seem to fit. I recognise one of them. It's Sweeney, the leader of the group we ambushed when we first met Daymu. He sees me looking and grins, showing his toothless gums.

Finally, everyone is ordered to stand. Tusker walks through the door, closely followed by Ramage. The scar down the side of Tusker's face looks like a claw mark. He stands to attention, his gaze locked on Kas. He flicks his tongue in and out like a lizard.

Ramage shuffles in, his attention directed at a wad of papers in his hands. He wears a pair of glasses that slide down his nose, and he pushes them back up with a finger. He sits, and Tusker gives the signal for everyone in the courtroom to do the same.

Ramage leans back in his chair, removes his glasses and looks across the short space between us. He rolls his shoulder and I remember it's where Harry shot him last year.

He's taking his time, showing who's in charge. He turns and whispers something to Tusker, who nods. They both smile, sharing some joke.

Tusker rises to his feet and sticks his chest out. 'This court is now in session,' he says. 'Commissioner Ramage presiding. Who comes before the court?' He must be remembering the lines from some old movie.

Jackson stands. 'Two accused collaborators, Your Honour,' he says. 'Captured by one of our patrols on the coast near Megs Creek. They were harbouring these two runaway Sileys.' He points to Kas and Daymu.

Ramage has put his glasses back on and now he peers over the top of them. 'Stand up,' he says.

It's hard to get up with our hands tied, so Murphy pulls us to our feet. My stomach is turning over, but I try to look Ramage in the eyes.

'What are your names?' he asks.

'You know who we are,' I say.

Tusker snaps at me. 'Show some respect in the commissioner's court. Answer the question!'

Ramage is unfussed. It's pretty clear he's going to pretend our meeting last night never happened. He shifts in his seat, massaging his shoulder with his hand. He waits.

'Finn Morrison,' I say.

Ramage turns to Tusker, holding back a laugh. 'We may need an interpreter here. Can you understand a word this boy is saying?' he says.

'Must be some sort of dog language, Your Honour,' Tusker replies, like he's never heard me speak before. He shifts his attention back to me. 'Try. To. Speak. English,' he says slowly and the guards all laugh.

'Thank you, deputy,' Ramage says. 'And who are you?' he

asks, looking at JT.

JT stands with his feet apart, staring him down. 'Jeremy Tutton,' he says. It's the first time I've heard his actual name.

Ramage nods. His voice is controlled, almost friendly. 'Where are you two from?'

'You know that, too,' I say. 'The town you chased Rose into last year.'

Tusker nods at our guards and I feel a blow to my kidneys. I've got no way of breaking my fall. I hit the boards face first and feel the stitches on my chin split open. Big hands lift me to my feet and the blood drips onto my shirt.

'Now,' Ramage says. 'I'll ask that question again. Where are you from?'

'Angowrie,' I say.

He snorts. 'A quarantined area!'

'It's where I was born.'

'So were lots of others but it didn't stop them leaving. It's a forbidden zone.'

'Didn't stop you from going there,' I say.

Jackson yanks me by the cable ties, but Ramage tells him to stop.

'I went there to reclaim my legal property—the Siley, Warda,' he says. 'I had every right to pursue her. But you'—he takes a deep breath before continuing—'you hid her and endangered her unborn child.'

I've heard this argument before, when I held Ramage at gunpoint in the valley. It still makes me seethe.

Now he braces himself against the edge of the table. 'You

kept her from the medical treatment she needed. You're lucky you're not being charged with murder as well.'

'Murder?' I say. 'You'd know all about that.'

Ramage simply smiles and waves his hand like he's brushing away flies. I look to our guards but they seem unconcerned by what they're hearing.

'Rose wanted her baby to be free,' I say.

'Free!' Ramage raises his voice a couple of notches. 'No Siley can be free. They're the property of their owners, and only their owners can make the decisions about their wellbeing.'

'I don't agree with that,' I say.

Ramage lets out an exaggerated laugh and bangs his hand on the table. 'Oh,' he says. '*You don't agree.*' He looks around the room. 'Well, let's throw out all the laws of the land and we'll consult young Finn Morrison whenever we want to make a decision. But we'll need some sort of code for this dogboy— like one bark for yes, two barks no!'

The Wilders and soldiers laugh along with him until he stops them with another wave of his hand. Tusker hasn't taken his eyes off Kas.

Ramage looks down at his papers. 'And these two, sergeant?' he asks, pointing to Kas and Daymu.

'Sileys, Your Honour,' Jackson says. 'Escapees guilty of crimes against free settlers. They have colluded with guerilla groups, murdered innocent patrollers and caused serious injury to Deputy Commissioner Tusker.'

Everyone's attention is drawn to Tusker, who parts the hair on his chin to reveal the scar where Kas cut him.

'Unfortunately,' Ramage continues, 'these two slaves are not on trial today. But I have a special interest in the one with the birthmark. She killed my son, Raymond.' He pauses and crosses himself. 'May he rest in peace.'

'Don't think it's peaceful where he's gone,' JT says.

Ramage ignores him. 'These Sileys will be punished when they are handed to the authorities in Wentworth.'

Kas lets out a muffled wail from behind the tape.

Ramage seems to consider something, then tells Sweeney to remove the tape from Kas's mouth. He peels it off roughly and Kas moves her jaw around to flex the muscles.

'State your full name,' Ramage demands.

'Kashmala,' she says.

'Your *full* name,' he says again.

Kas remains silent.

Ramage is breathing heavily, struggling to control himself, now. 'Your surname is the name of your owner, Siley. It's Ramage.'

'My surname is my father's: Afridi.'

'You see,' Ramage says, turning back to us. 'This is why Sileys can never assimilate. They hang onto their old lives. They infiltrate societies like ours—where the rule of law applies—and they try to drag us back into their tribal ways. This,' he continues, banging his fist on the table for emphasis, 'is why we must use a firm hand, teach them respect.'

Kas can't help herself. 'Respect!' she screams. 'Murder, rape, torture, slavery—is that what you call respect?'

'Put the tape back on this animal,' Ramage yells.

Tusker moves quickly across the room and wraps his arms around Kas from behind. His hands grab at her breasts as Sweeney takes a roll of tape from his bag and winds it around her head and mouth. She struggles to breathe.

'Get them out of my courtroom,' Ramage yells.

Tusker is reluctant to let go of Kas, but Sweeney and one of the other Wilders pull her and Daymu away and drag them out of the court. I watch on helpless, and then they're gone.

Quiet falls on the room again. Ramage tidies the papers on his desk and Tusker struts back to his chair.

'Finn Morrison. Jeremy Tutton,' Ramage wheezes. 'Stand up.'

We struggle to our feet.

'The rebuilding of our society relies on the establishment of order. You have chosen to betray your country by disrupting that order and endangering the lives of others. Sileys are slaves, they always have been. They do not have rights and nor should they. Their lower intellect makes them good for only one thing—work.' He pauses to allow everyone to consider that statement. 'You are both charged with harbouring fugitive Sileys and perverting the course of justice. We find you guilty on both charges.'

'What?' JT says. 'We haven't had the chance to defend ourselves.'

'Defend yourselves?' Tusker interrupts. 'You were caught red-handed with Sileys. You have no defence.'

Ramage coughs violently, doubling over and trying to catch his breath. When he straightens again, he continues. 'I sentence you to reclassification.' He turns, pushes himself away from the table and leaves through the back door.

'What does that mean?' I call after him.

Tusker stands slowly and walks around the table. He makes a *tsk tsk* sound with his tongue and shakes his head. '*Ooh*,' he says, drawing the word out. 'Reclassification is a very special punishment. Can't you guess what it might be?'

Angela mentioned being reclassified because her parents had been immigrants. But that can't apply to us.

Tusker pulls up a chair and leans in towards us. 'You have to be very special to be reclassified,' he says. 'Very special indeed.'

'Our parents weren't migrants. They were born here and so were we,' I say.

'Do you have birth certificates to prove that?' he asks.

'You know that's impossible.'

He shrugs his shoulders. 'So, you have no way of proving your status.'

It's pointless arguing with him.

'What happens to us, now?' JT asks.

'Well, since you seem to like them so much, you're going to become Sileys. You'll be implanted with tracking devices and sent to Wentworth.' He sways closer to me before adding, 'Nowhere near your girlfriends though, I'll see to that.' He winks at me.

'You can't do that!' JT says.

'Oh, we can do it,' Tusker replies. 'And you know what the best bit is?' He pauses, waiting for us to guess. 'Now that you're Sileys, we get to collect a bounty for each of you.'

The whole time Tusker's talking I'm looking at the soldiers, trying to read their reactions. Why are they allowing this to happen?

'You call this justice?' I say to Jackson. 'Can't you see what's happening here?'

But he barely looks at me. 'Not our problem, kid.'

When they escort us from the courtroom, out the front door, Kas and Daymu are gone.

10

We lose track of time in the cell, dozing on and off through the heat of the day and shivering at night. The cut on my chin has formed a scab and it's hard not to pick at it. Days go by, marked only by the arrival of our meals of beans and stale bread. The beans are lukewarm and swim in some sort of soupy liquid but we can soften the bread by dipping it. It feels like my body is shrinking with the lack of food. All through the summer we ate well—rabbits and abalone and fish, veggies from the garden. That seems like years ago.

We pace the cell to keep ourselves active. I try to distract myself from fretting about Kas by thinking of us back at the point, our clothes in a pile on the beach, diving into the deepest pool and holding our breath until our lungs are ready to burst. But every time I try to picture this, the image is overtaken by Kas arriving at the courthouse, wild-eyed and frantic, her face swollen and her mouth taped. What sort of damage has been done to her now?

The sound of a key in the lock jolts me into the present. Two guards we haven't seen before block the light in the doorway. 'You,' they say, pointing to me. 'On your feet.'

They lead me along the corridor to the room where we first met Angela. It's been at least two weeks, maybe more, since the trial. I'm pushed through the door. Angela stands by a stainless-steel trolley, laying out instruments and putting on latex gloves. This time one of the guards stays in the room.

'Hey,' she says to me. 'How you feeling?'

I can only shake my head.

'Give me a look at that chin.'

I sit down and she checks the cut. 'I'll have to stitch it again,' she says.

She takes a wet piece of gauze and begins to dab at the wound. She does her best to dissolve the scab but it catches on the old stitches as she pulls them out. My whole face feels hot and my eyes are watering.

Again, she stitches the wound. Again, it hurts like shit.

There's a knock at the door and the guard steps outside.

Angela leans in closer like she's checking the cut. She looks over my shoulder, then slips something into my mouth and touches her finger to her lips.

'I'm going to put a tracker in your hand,' she says, her voice barely a whisper. 'It's a dud. The live one is in your mouth. It's up to you how you play it from here.'

'Thank you,' I say. Though I can't figure out what she means yet. 'Have you seen Kas and Daymu?' I ask.

'I saw them after the trial. They'd been in a fight. They're tough, those two.'

The guard steps halfway through the door, but his back is turned and he's talking to someone outside.

Angela keeps her eyes on him and talks fast and low. 'They've been transported to Wentworth. Kas said...' She hesitates.

'What?'

'She said not to try to follow them.'

'She would say that.'

'It's good advice. Wentworth is even more dangerous now that you're Sileys.'

'Everywhere is dangerous,' I say.

She forces a quick smile. 'Things are changing, Finn. The army's growing tired of Ramage.'

The guard steps into the room and stands over us. 'Get on with it,' he says, his hand on the gun in his holster.

Angela lifts my left hand and lays it palm down on the top of the trolley. Then she slides open a drawer and takes out something that looks like a staple gun. She inserts a small black square of plastic about a quarter the size of a matchbox into the chamber. My tongue touches the piece she hid in my mouth. It's the same. 'This is going to hurt,' she says. She squeezes the trigger and pain shoots up my arm. I reel away and jam my hand under my armpit.

'Sorry,' she says. 'It's not my choice to do this.'

'All right,' the guard interrupts. 'Enough of that bullshit.' He picks me up by the arm and pulls me towards the door.

'Stay safe,' Angela says.

'Have you seen Rowdy?' I call back. But the door closes and I don't hear her answer.

When I get to the cell, JT is taken away.

I pull the live tracker from my mouth and slip it into my pocket, then flex my fingers to try to get some movement into my hand. The implant forms a red lump and blood trickles from the entry point. I knead it with my fingertips and brace myself to try and force it out the way it went in. But it feels like it has wire arms pushing outwards, holding it in place.

Five minutes later, the door opens and JT is shoved through. Like me, he's holding the back of his hand and wincing with the pain. 'Shit!' he says. 'That's as bad as the branding.'

I wait until the door has been closed and bolted before shuffling over to him. 'Did Angela say anything to you?' I whisper.

'No. The guard was with us the whole time,' he says. He opens his mouth and shows me the tracker sitting on his tongue. 'But I'm guessing you can explain this.'

I tell him what Angela said.

'So, the ones in our hands don't work,' JT says.

'Nope, but they'll think they do as long as we keep the active ones on us.'

'But if we escape, we ditch the live ones?'

We both take a few seconds to try to figure out what sort of advantage this gives us.

'At least we know one thing,' I say. 'The tracking devices are active.'

'It still doesn't make sense,' JT says. 'They only have electricity for a few hours a day, as best we can tell. Tracking like this is done by satellite. But you have to have a home base to connect to. And that needs electricity to run.'

'Maybe they can only track for short periods each day,' I say.

'It's possible. Problem is, we don't know when they have power and when they don't.'

'We'd know if we were in Wentworth,' I say.

I tell JT about Kas's message. 'It's not like we have a choice, is it?' he says. 'They're going to take us there anyway.'

Three days later, in the middle of the afternoon, we're loaded onto the truck. No one tells us where we are going, but we drive through Longley this time, out onto the highway towards Wentworth. We've hidden the live trackers in the seams of our shirts.

Grey clouds roll in and there's rain coming. The humidity is high and it's like a sauna under the tarpaulin on the back of the truck. JT and I are cable-tied behind our backs but not bound together.

We have three guards: Murphy and Jackson from the courthouse, and Sweeney, who's come along to collect the bounty and return it to Ramage. He's acting cocky, telling the soldiers about the number of Sileys he's captured.

'They're easy pickings for experienced hunters,' he says to Jackson.

The soldier doesn't seem interested.

I laugh. 'Yeah, easy pickings,' I say. 'Last time we saw you, you were tied up like a Christmas turkey, hopping around without your boots.'

A smile passes between the two soldiers.

'Ah, so our young friend has found his voice,' Sweeney says, smiling to show his gums. 'That is a voice is it—that growling and grunting noise?

'Stop it,' JT says. 'That smile of yours is blinding me. What toothpaste do you use? I've gotta get myself some.'

Sweeney moves to kick JT, but Jackson reaches out and grabs him by the arm. 'Sit down,' he barks.

Sweeney shrugs the hand away. 'That mouth is going to get you in trouble one day,' he says to JT.

'Oh, you mean my mouth full of teeth,' JT says with an exaggerated smile.

'I'll smash them down your fuckin' throat if you're not careful,' Sweeney snarls.

The truck is slow and lumbering. After an hour or so, we pull over and the flap is lifted at the back. 'Have to check the motor,' the driver calls. 'We're losing power.'

'Piss stop, then,' Murphy says.

We slide carefully down, landing on our feet in the gravel by the side of the road.

'We can't piss tied up like this,' JT says.

'Cut the ties, Murph,' Jackson says. 'We don't want them

pissing their pants in the truck.'

'You sure?' Murphy asks.

'Where are they gonna run?' Jackson says, sweeping his arm to take in the country around us. The road stretches out in either direction, the railway line running parallel as far as the eye can see. The plains spread out under a haze of low cloud and mist rising off the paddocks. The air is thick and still. To the south the hills rise towards heavily treed ridges, fold after fold, until they merge with the hanging cloud. I wonder whether there are watchers up there somewhere, looking down on us and trying to figure out why this truck has stopped where it has.

The cable ties are cut, and JT and I wander to the side of the road to piss. He's scanning the tree line, too. 'Get the feeling we're being watched?' he whispers.

'Yeah.'

A hissing noise erupts behind us and we turn to see steam shooting out from under the truck.

'What the—?' Jackson says.

The driver has been looking underneath. Now, he reaches behind the cabin and undoes a series of clips before tipping it forward to expose the motor.

'Useless piece of shit,' he says. 'I told 'em the cooling system was leaking.'

Jackson is on edge, a finger on the trigger of his rifle and his eyes darting about. 'Not a place we want to be stuck,' he says, looking up to the hills. 'What's your name, soldier?' he asks the driver.

'Winston, sir,' he replies. He's young, maybe only in his

early twenties, thin and rangy, with a shadow of whiskers on his chin.

'How serious is it?' he asks, nodding towards the truck.

'Not sure. I'm not a mechanic.'

Sweeney reaches behind his back and pulls a gun from under his shirt. Jackson swings his rifle towards him, but Sweeney throws his hands in the air. 'Whoa, whoa,' he says, a jitter in his voice. 'Just for protection.'

'Put it away,' Jackson says.

Sweeney eyes me with a smile and pushes the gun back into his belt.

Horizontal lightning sheets across the plain. A few seconds later, thunder grumbles in reply. A thin rain starts to fall. The afternoon is wearing on—the dim outline of the sun is barely visible through the clouds to the west.

The three soldiers huddle in front of the truck speaking in low voices. Jackson points up towards the ridge.

'I know motors,' JT calls to them. 'Worked on them all the time on the farm.'

Jackson walks over to us. He lifts JT's chin with the barrel of his rifle and moves in closer. 'Truck engines?' he asks.

'Tractors, mostly,' JT says, trying to keep his voice calm. 'But a motor's a motor.'

'He's lying,' Sweeney spits. 'Why would he fix it?'

The soldier jerks his rifle so JT is standing on tiptoes. 'Because if he doesn't, I'm going to shoot him,' he says. 'Bounty or no bounty.' To reinforce his point, he slams his fist into JT's stomach, dropping him to his knees.

JT gasps for breath. When he can speak again he says, 'Do you want me to fix it or not?'

Jackson looks at Murphy and Winston, then Sweeney. They're not convinced, but they don't have much choice. Jackson jerks his rifle towards the truck and says, 'Try anything and I'll kill you without a second thought.'

Sweeney is clearly pissed off, but he stays quiet.

It's a little victory and JT knows it. He swaggers past Sweeney and gives him a wink. The more I see of JT, the more he reminds me of kids I knew at school—the smartarses with the confidence to pull it off. They joked with the teachers, got them onside then went ahead and did what they liked.

JT leans over the engine, has a quick look then climbs underneath to check it from another angle. There's no steam visible anymore, but there's a continuous hissing noise coming from somewhere towards the front of the motor.

'A hose clamp's come loose at the back of the radiator,' JT says. 'We got any tools?'

Winston pulls open a metal box attached to the tray. 'What do you need?' he says.

'Multigrips and a Phillips-head screwdriver,' JT calls back.

Murphy takes the tools from Winston and crawls under the truck. 'I'll be watching everything you do,' he says to JT.

'No worries, fat fella, but give me some elbow room, will you,' JT says.

I hear a yelp. Murphy must have kicked him.

It takes a few minutes but eventually the two of them slide out and stand up. JT gives me a look I can't interpret. 'We need to top up the radiator,' he says. 'Otherwise we're going nowhere.'

'We've only got our water bottles,' Jackson says. 'I'm guessing that won't be enough?'

'Not even close,' JT replies.

Jackson looks around warily. 'We passed a dam a little way back,' he says. 'Winston, what have you got we can carry water in?'

Winston reaches into a compartment behind the cabin and pulls out a fuel container. It's full and he staggers under its weight. He opens the cap on the top of the fuel tank and begins to pour.

The rain has become heavier. Visibility has dropped and the thunder is coming closer. I reckon there's only a couple of hours of daylight left. Murphy is getting fidgety too—there's sweat pouring down his face. 'How do we do this?' he asks Jackson.

'You and Winston head back to the dam, quick as you can. Run if you have to. I'll stay here with the prisoners and—what was your name again?'

'Sweeney.'

'Sweeney, the toothless hunter,' JT chips in.

'Shut up, kid,' Jackson yells. 'Sweeney, you stay here.' He pokes a finger into Sweeney's chest. 'And I haven't forgotten about that gun of yours.'

'Oh, I'm staying, all right,' Sweeney spits. 'I'm not letting these two out of my sight.'

The soldiers set out along the road, Winston carrying the fuel can and Murphy struggling to keep up. Jackson orders us into the truck. At least it's dry under the tarp. In the confusion, they've forgotten to tie our hands. Sweeney watches us. This is an important job for him, transporting two prisoners, collecting the bounty and returning to Longley. He plays with the gun in his hands, spinning it on one finger like a gunslinger. He's enjoying himself.

Jackson eyes him warily, but says nothing.

An hour passes. The light is fading, a combination of the thickening rain and the dropping sun. Eventually Jackson jumps out and we hear his boots as he paces up and down.

Sweeney leans in to us and says, 'If anything happens here, any of your rebel mates turn up, you're the first two I'm going to shoot.'

'Shoot us and there'll be no bounty,' I say. 'What would Ramage say about that?'

'He'd say a dead collaborator is better than one roaming the countryside causing havoc,' he says.

'The only people causing havoc are Wilders like you,' I say.

He smiles. 'You know the difference between you and me? This.' He holds his gun in front of my face. 'And, unlike you, I've got the guts to use it.'

Jackson's head appears at the back. 'Shut up in there.' He strains forward, staring out along the road. 'You hear that?' he asks.

We all listen. Above the beating of the rain on the tarp I pick up a faint sound. It's muffled by the thickness of the air but I'm certain it's a diesel engine. Slowly it becomes louder until the lights of another truck appear over a small crest in the road.

11

There's nothing cautious about the way the truck approaches—
it doesn't slow until it's almost on us. It pulls up alongside with
a hiss of air brakes. The stench of livestock fills the air. I hear
a door open and a muffled conversation. Sweeney leans out
the back, trying to figure out what's going on.

The rain is belting down now, and we can't hear anything
of what's happening outside. JT whispers urgently, 'Give me
your tracker.'

'Why?'

'Don't argue.'

I inch the tracker out of the lining of my shirt and pass it to him. Just then Jackson orders us out of the truck. Sweeney is suspicious and keeps his gun where we can see it.

On the road, there are two more soldiers. They pull jackets over their heads to protect themselves from the rain. The cattle truck has picked up Murphy and Winston, who are now pouring water into the radiator. When it's full, they cap it again. Winston pulls the cabin back into position and climbs in. He turns the motor over and it takes.

Suddenly, JT drops to the ground and scuttles under the second truck. He pauses briefly then slides all the way through and out the other side. Before he can get more than a few metres the two soldiers tackle him to the ground and one of them sits on his back.

Sweeney is quickly beside them, keeping an eye on his property. 'Don't hurt him,' he yells. 'I need that bounty.'

JT is hauled to his feet. Sweeney is in his face. 'You're so much dumber than I thought, kid. Where were you going to go? And how far would you get with this?' He grabs JT's hand and turns it round to show the implanted tracker.

The cattle truck moves off, the glow of its tail lights gradually fading into the distance. We climb into the tray and Winston starts to grind through the gears. We pick up speed but we've only gone another ten minutes when the engine coughs and cuts out. We keep rolling as Winston tries to restart the motor, but eventually we come to a halt. This time there's the sound of water gushing onto the road, along with the familiar hissing of steam.

Murphy grabs JT by the shirt and shakes him. 'What have you done?'

JT is all innocence and wonder. 'Don't look at me. You were watching. I fixed the clamp back on and tightened it far as it'd go.'

Murphy pushes him back against the metal ribbing holding the tarp.

'That'll do, Murph,' Jackson barks. Then, looking at JT and me, 'Stay here! Don't move!' He jumps out the back.

The gloom has turned to dark and the rain has eased to a thin drizzle. The night seems to close in on us prematurely. We hear shuffling under the cabin and plenty of swearing. After a few minutes, Jackson and Winston climb in with us.

'It's not the clamp,' Winston says. 'The hose has split.'

Murphy looks at JT as though somehow he's still to blame but eventually drops his gaze. As for JT, he seems pretty pleased with himself.

'We've got no choice,' Jackson says. 'We'll have to wait here. There's another truck coming through tomorrow. In the meantime, we sit tight.'

Sweeney is not impressed. 'What sort of operation are you running here? You're supposed to be the army! You can't even keep your machinery going.'

'I don't know whether you've noticed,' Jackson shoots back, 'but resources are stretched. We have to take three trucks apart to cobble one together.'

'And hasn't that worked well for you?' Sweeney can't keep the sneer from his voice.

'Easy for you to say,' Murphy cuts in. 'You Wilders answer to no one. We know what you've been doing these past two years.'

106

'Doing?' Sweeney spits. 'You mean keeping order while you lot hide away in Wentworth, too afraid to venture out and help us.'

'Yeah, you've kept order,' Murphy says. 'But your methods would be illegal in any sort of civilised society.'

'We haven't had a civilised society since the virus,' Sweeney says, his voice getting more arrogant by the minute. 'We do what we have to.'

'Bullshit!' I can't help myself. I've been listening to them argue as though we're not here. I pull up my shirt sleeve and show the branded R on my arm. 'You *had* to do that, did you? Brand kids like cattle. Murphy's right, you're animals and one day you'll face the law.'

Sweeney laughs. 'The law?' he says. 'We *are* the law. I thought you'd understand that by now.'

Jackson has heard enough. 'All right, that'll do,' he snaps. 'I'll take first watch.' He slips off into the darkness.

The night is still and quiet, apart from the crunching of gravel under Jackson's feet as he circles the truck again and again. The only other sound is the occasional birdcall—the hoot of a barn owl or the call of a nightjar. We try to get comfortable but the metal tray makes it impossible. I doze, waking when Jackson swaps sentry duty with Murphy.

'Anything?' Murphy asks as they clamber around each other.

'Nothing,' Jackson says. 'But stay alert.'

I must have dropped off again but I'm woken by a louder birdcall—a high-pitched whistle like a hawk.

Hawks don't hunt at night.

I nudge JT, but he's already awake. He takes my hand and guides it to his hip. I feel the outline of a screwdriver in his pocket. The others don't seem to have noticed the call. Only Sweeney is awake, watching us.

I can't hear Murphy outside. He might be sitting in the cabin.

The deep silence of the night is broken by the sudden rip of an arrow piercing the tarp behind Sweeney's head. He ducks and sprawls on the floor.

'Murph?' Jackson calls.

There's no reply.

'You okay, Murph?' he calls again.

Silence.

Jackson and Winston grab JT and me, holding their weapons at our heads and forcing us towards the open end of the truck. My heart is hammering at a million miles an hour and if there was any food in my stomach I'd throw it up.

There's no sound or movement outside. We wait a minute, then Jackson edges us off the tray, using us as shields. The air is cooler out here and everything is damp from the rain. The moon throws a dull light from behind thinning cloud. We're marched around the truck, our guards panicked and peering into the night, Sweeney staying close. They check the cabin but he's not there. Sweeney is doing full circles now, his gun pointed into the dark.

'Murph,' Jackson yells. 'Where are ya?'

A breeze has picked up and finally the clouds shift from the moon, bathing us in light.

'Murph,' he tries again.

'Your friend won't be coming back,' calls a voice I know.

We all swing around and there, on top of the railway embankment, his face shining in the moonlight, stands Tahir.

Jackson and Winston raise their rifles towards him, while Sweeney grabs me around the neck and pushes the barrel of his revolver into my cheek.

Tahir's voice is calm. 'You are surrounded. Put down your guns.'

'Where's Murphy,' Jackson demands.

Tahir takes his time to reply. 'Gone,' he says.

Jackson makes a move towards Tahir, his rifle raised to his shoulder, but he barely takes two steps before a shot cracks the air and he falls to the ground. At the same time JT throws himself at Sweeney, who screams and staggers towards the truck. Winston lowers his weapon and drops it. Sweeney is writhing on the road, his hands clutching at the screwdriver buried in his thigh. JT has grabbed Sweeney's revolver and stands over him.

'Dumber than you thought, huh?' JT says.

No-landers appear from every side. Gabriel walks towards me smiling grimly. He's wearing sunglasses. 'We meet again,' he says.

I'm surprised to see Afa, whose friend Kaylo was killed by Tahir. 'Lucky you broke down here,' Afa says.

'Not luck,' JT says.

'What do you mean?' I ask.

'When I was fixing the hose I used a bit of hot metal to burn slits in it. This truck was never going to make it to Wentworth.'

He smiles, happy with his handiwork.

Winston is still on the ground, his hands on the back of his head, while Sweeney has propped himself up against one of the tyres. He takes a deep breath and yanks the screwdriver out of his leg. Blood spreads from the wound.

'What now?' I ask Tahir, who has come down off the bank.

'We are only interested in the truck,' Tahir says. He turns to JT. 'Is it repairable?'

'No, it's stuffed. I reckon they cooked the motor.'

Tahir is disappointed. 'Were they taking you to Wentworth?' he asks.

'Yeah. They captured us down on the coast,' I say.

He looks at me with contempt. 'It seems you make a habit of getting caught.'

Gabriel puts his hand on Tahir's shoulder. 'Easy, brother,' he says. 'We don't need more enemies than we already have.' It's not the first time I've seen Gabriel play the peacemaker.

Tahir shifts his attention to the truck, climbing into the cabin and feeling around under the dashboard. He finds a box of bullets and climbs back down. 'Not a total waste of time,' he says, rattling the box. He has Murphy's rifle and now he snatches Sweeney's gun from JT.

Gabriel takes me aside and Afa joins us. 'We heard about the battle in the valley, the defeat of Ramage,' Gabriel says.

'How did you hear about that?' I ask.

They look at each other. 'Tell you later,' Afa says. 'We need to sort out this truck.' He finds another fuel container and he and Gabriel disappear under the chassis. We hear the gush of liquid and the smell of diesel fills the air. They pass the container to Tahir who walks around the vehicle splashing the fuel on the tarp and into the cabin.

The rest of us retreat. Sweeney struggles to his feet and he and Winston are led away at gunpoint. Tahir dips a rag in diesel before striking a match and setting it alight. He throws it into the cabin and the whole interior is quickly engulfed in flames. We back away as the heat reaches us, mesmerised by the leaping flames and the plume of black smoke billowing over the embankment. Jackson's body lies where he fell.

Afa, Gabriel and Tahir are the only No-landers I recognise, though a couple look vaguely familiar from the raid on the feedstore last year. I don't see any of the kids who were at the No-landers' property when Kas and I escaped.

'Let's go,' Tahir eventually says, turning his back on the burning truck and beginning the climb towards the ridge.

'What about these two,' Afa asks, pointing his rifle at Sweeney and Winston.

Tahir stops and walks back to the two prisoners. 'This one is useless,' he says, pointing at Sweeney. 'He'll only slow us down.'

Afa blindfolds Winston and drags him away.

In one swift, deliberate motion, Tahir steps towards Sweeney, stands over him and shoots him in the chest.

It's like all the oxygen is sucked from the air and I can't breathe. I reel with the shock of it and grab JT's arm. Tahir shrugs and walks away. The glow of the fire lights the faces of the other No-landers and I see fear in them all.

We catch up to Winston, who must have heard the shot.

His head moves frantically from side to side and his arms are stretched out in front of him, groping in the dark. Afa pushes him forward.

As far as we can tell, the No-landers think JT and I will go with them, though no one's paying any attention to us. We hesitate halfway up the hill, trying to make one of those quick decisions that can change everything later. 'What do you reckon?' JT asks.

'We've gotta get clear of this truck. It'll draw soldiers or Wilders, or both,' I say.

JT nods. 'But once we have, I'm getting as far away from Tahir as I can.'

'Me too.'

The No-landers are most of the way up the hill before JT and I start after them. The paddock is steep and the grass slippery from the rain. Bracken fern has crept out of the bush to reclaim the pasture and it's waist high by the time we enter the trees. Moonlight filters through the canopy, allowing us to jog without tripping over fallen branches or stumbling into blackberries.

Eventually, a rocky outcrop appears ahead of us. Gabriel has waited and he directs us into a gap between the largest boulders. We squeeze through and follow him to an area enclosed by rock walls. It's about the size of my backyard at home. One side is covered by a large blue tarp, held in place by rough poles and ropes. There's bedding, water containers and cooking gear strewn under it, while in the middle there's a stone circle around the remains of a fire.

The No-landers sit with their backs to the walls. Winston squats on the ground. He must have fallen on the way up—a cut on his cheek trickles blood onto his uniform.

Tahir paces up and down. 'We rest here,' he says. 'Then pack the camp and move at dawn.'

Food is passed around, meat that might be kangaroo or wallaby. It's cold and hardly cooked, but right now we'd eat pretty much anything.

Everything has happened so quickly tonight—the truck breaking down, the ambush, Murphy disappearing, Jackson and Sweeney shot—and now this. We're free, but the thought of being involved with the No-landers puts me on edge. We have to get to Wentworth.

Afa sits with us. He takes my left hand and turns it over. 'So, you're one of us now,' he says.

This draws Tahir's attention. 'Do you know if the trackers are active?' he asks.

'They still need power and from what we can make out they only have it for a few hours a day,' I say.

'As we thought,' Tahir says. 'It's why we must keep moving. By the time they get a patrol to where they think we are, we're gone.'

'Why is the army working with the Wilders?' Afa asks.

'You know about the zones?' I say.

'Yes.'

'The army can't control the zones on their own, so they let people like Ramage do what they like as long as they maintain order and keep the farms producing.'

'But surely,' Tahir says, 'they can see how corrupt he is. He rules by force.'

'Like you,' JT interrupts.

I wish JT would shut up. He always seems to want to provoke and his mouth is going to cost us at some stage.

'We don't rule,' Tahir spits. 'We survive.' He turns his back and walks away.

'What do you know about the valley farm?' I ask Afa.

'We haven't been there ourselves,' he says. 'Too dangerous.'

I get the feeling there's something he's not telling us. He walks over to Gabriel and they have a short conversation. Gabriel strokes his chin, thinking, deciding. Finally, he nods and Afa disappears through a gap in the rocks.

A couple of minutes later, he re-emerges with another, smaller, No-lander. He's wearing a hoodie that shadows his face. Before I can work out what's happening he lunges at me, dropping to his knees. The hood pushes back to show a smooth round face and a shock of dirty blonde curls.

Willow.

12

'Finn!' Her voice is familiar but somehow different. Older. Her face is smudged with charcoal in lines across her cheeks, and her hands are rough and calloused where she grips my arm.

The questions spill out of her. 'How did you get here? Where have you come from? Where's Kas? What about Rowdy?'

'Whoa, whoa,' I say. 'One at a time.'

JT has never met Willow but he's heard enough about her to know who she is.

'What are you doing here?' Willow asks again.

'It's a long story, Wils. We've got a lot of catching up to do. But, what about you? How come you're here with this lot?'

She shakes her head. 'Ah, Finn,' she says. 'It's so good to see you.'

This time she pulls away and gets herself together. She tells the story like she's rehearsed it. 'Ramage sent Wilders to the valley to steal Hope, but Mum had hidden with her in the underground shelter we'd built over the summer.'

'What happened to you?' I ask.

'I was...' She pauses. 'I was picking blackberries. I didn't get the warning. When they couldn't find Hope they took me instead.'

'Where was Harry?' I ask.

'Hunting,' she says, swallowing hard.

'But how did you get here? Did you escape?'

'We were travelling on foot. Camping in the bush, staying off the roads. The Wilders were scared of the No-landers.' She glances at Afa, who smiles. 'There was a huge storm one night,' she continues. 'I took my chance and ran.'

She looks at the ground and brushes one hand through her hair. 'It was crazy—lightning and thunder and shouting and screaming. I tried to find my way home but I got lost.'

'We found her,' Afa says. 'She was half-dead. Cuts and scratches all over her. She didn't say a word for the first week.'

'Afa,' Willow says, nodding at him. 'He looks after me. Keeps me safe.'

'Bullshit!' Afa says, turning to me with a broad smile. 'She looks after herself. Have you seen what she can do with a bow and arrow?'

Willow turns to me and raises her eyebrows. I remember

the hours she practised in the backyard at Angowrie, shooting at a target on an old mattress.

'Was that you who shot through the canopy on the truck?' JT asks.

She nods. 'But, Finn,' she says. 'Where's Kas?'

I settle back against the rock and tell her everything that's happened since we left the valley last spring—or at least as much as she needs to know. She fumes when she hears about Tusker cutting my chin and swears under her breath when I get to the trial. Afa listens intently, too. I don't mention anything about Angela or the dud trackers she implanted.

Telling our story to Willow makes our need to rescue Kas and Daymu feel even more urgent. I have no idea how to go about finding them in Wentworth—everything to this point has been out of our control—but at least now we won't be going there as prisoners. And maybe there are others trying to do the same as us—find the ones they love.

The night is wearing on. The No-landers bed down under the tarp, but Willow stays with me and JT. She's still full of questions, but tiredness has caught up with me and I can't find the energy to answer them. Eventually we lie down, huddling together. Willow is behind me, one arm around my waist. I know it's comforting for her, and it's reassuring for me too.

The camp stirs with the first sign of dawn. The No-landers are packing their gear and folding the tarp. It's been an uncomfortable night and, in the haze of being only half-awake, it takes me a while to piece together what's happened and why we're here.

The preparations are interrupted by a voice from above us, high on the largest boulder. 'Tahir,' it calls. 'Quick!'

Willow, JT and I follow as Tahir slides between the rock faces before climbing a series of ledges that lead to the top.

A tall No-lander lies flat on the rock, a pair of binoculars pressed to his eyes. He passes them to Tahir.

We're above the treetops here, with a clear view out to the highway and the plains beyond. It's growing lighter by the minute allowing us to pick out more detail in the stretch between us and the road. The truck is now a black shell, the telltale smoke allowing us to pinpoint it easily. The grass is scorched around it but the wet ground must have stopped the fire from spreading any further. I reckon we're three hundred metres from it. But that's not what's drawing our attention. Another truck has pulled up and men are climbing out of the back.

Tahir hands me the binoculars. It takes a few seconds to focus, but when I do, my heart stops. They're not soldiers— they're Wilders. There is a dozen of them and at the front, pointing up towards the ridge we're on, stands Tusker. As their truck begins a laboured U-turn, half the men fan out, moving into the paddock while the rest, led by Tusker, head straight for us.

There's no need for talk, we slide down and get back to the others. The No-landers have hidden their camping gear. They have nothing but rifles over their shoulders and they're ready to run.

Tahir is barking orders. 'Split up,' he says. 'Head south, higher into the hills. Meet at the usual place in two days.'

'What about him?' one of the No-landers asks, pointing at Winston, who's cowering behind us, hoping not to be noticed.

'He is useless to us,' Tahir says. He draws Sweeney's pistol from his belt and waves it at JT and me, wanting a clear shot.

I can't explain why, but I hold my ground. JT does the same. So does Willow.

Tahir looks over his shoulder, checking to see if the others will back him, but they're all pushing through the passage, hurrying to escape. He speaks though gritted teeth. 'You have learnt nothing. These people are your enemies. They will hunt you down and kill you.'

He tries to step past us but we move quickly, keeping ourselves between him and Winston. Gabriel is the last No-lander to leave. It's the first time I've seen him this morning. He grabs Tahir by the arm and pulls him towards the passage. 'Come, brother,' he says. 'They are close.'

'Have it your way,' Tahir says, pointing the gun at me. 'But don't expect us to save you again.'

Tahir disappears through the gap as Winston steps out from behind us. Gabriel lingers. He lifts his sunglasses to rub his eyes with the back of his hand. His eyes are yellow. 'Stay safe,' he says, and then he's gone.

It takes us a few seconds to realise what we've seen. But right now, escape is more important.

'Which way, Wils?' I ask.

She doesn't hesitate, leading us in the opposite direction to the No-landers. There's a crack in the rock face a few inches wide. 'Watch where I put my feet,' she says. She wedges her hand into the gap, jams her foot in next to it and hauls herself upwards. She climbs like a monkey, repeating the same sequence before disappearing over the top. JT goes next. He struggles with the first section, which is the steepest, but makes it to Willow, who reaches down and pulls him up the last few metres.

I start to climb but my boots are too big to fit in the crack. Before I know what's happening, I feel hands under my foot, lifting me higher to where the crack widens and I can get some grip. I look down at Winston. 'Thanks,' I say.

He nods and gives me a thumbs-up sign. 'Good luck,' he says. 'You too.'

Willow directs us to the other side of the boulder we've climbed. It slopes into the undergrowth on the uphill side and we jump the last metre. JT and I are ready to head further into the trees when Willow says, 'No. This way.' She pushes through thick bracken fern at the base of the rock and into a hidden overhang. There are blankets and clothes on the ground in a space that just fits the three of us.

Willow puts a finger to her lips and we wait.

Within five minutes the bush is filled with sound, heavy foot-falls and men calling to each other. Someone jumps down off the rock and stands still for ages. I'm sure my heart is beating loud enough for him to hear.

'There!' A deep voice echoes off the rocks and men crash through the bush heading away from us. A gunshot cracks the air, then another. There are men yelling now. 'To your right, to your right. Three of them.'

'Shoot to kill,' Tusker calls. I'd recognise his voice anywhere.

It's not hard to track their progress, their voices gradually fading as they chase the No-landers higher into the forest. Eventually, the gunshots are just muffled echoes beyond the ridge.

Once it's quiet, we venture out from the overhang, staying low, and make our way along the rock face. My heart jumps into my mouth when a wallaby breaks cover and zigzags through the trees.

The forest beyond the outcrop is too thick to see any distance, so we stop and listen.

Nothing.

JT is the first to speak. 'I reckon we should climb up on the rock and see what we can see. Going downhill might be safest.'

We skirt around the eastern side that's in full sun now. Not wanting to risk getting trapped in the gap in the rock, Willow leads us up another way. She knows every crack and ledge.

When we reach the viewing area, we shimmy forward on our stomachs until we can see out to the plain.

The truck the Wilders arrived in has moved a few hundred metres back the way it came and now sits on the side of the road. A figure stands on the cabin roof. Binoculars glint in the morning sun. To the west, four figures walk down through the trees towards the truck. One is taller and thinner than the others—it's Winston. To the east, in the direction of Wentworth, the paddocks are clear.

We back away and sit looking at each other. The rock is already warm, even though the sun's only been up for an hour, and we know we're in for another hot day. There's no sign of the rain from yesterday.

'Wils,' I say. 'We're going to Wentworth to find Kas and Daymu.'

She doesn't hesitate. 'I'm coming with you.'

JT looks doubtful.

'Don't worry,' I say. 'She'll keep up.'

Willow looks pissed off that I even have to say this.

I remember Gabriel's yellow, crusty eyes. 'Wils, has Gabriel been sick?'

She looks at me, curious. 'He was out on the plain with a couple of others. When they came back their eyes were sore from the dust.'

'Have you been close to him? Touched him?'

'Why?'

'Just tell me. It's important.'

'No. Gabriel spent most of his time with Tahir.'

JT nods at me. 'Come on,' he says.

We're about to start the climb down when I remember something else. 'The live trackers?' I ask JT. 'Should we leave them here?'

'That'd be a bit hard,' he says. 'They'll be in Wentworth by now.'

'What do you mean?'

'You're a bit slow sometimes, Finn,' he says. He pauses while I try to figure it out.

It hits me. 'The other truck!' I say. 'That's what you were doing when you dived under it.'

He winks. 'Yep, two trackers heading straight for Wentworth, stuck up under the tray of a cattle truck. Every time they check, Finn Morrison and Jeremy Tutton will be in Wentworth. What'll really confuse them is when the truck does its next trip to Longley!'

Willow's got no idea what we're talking about. 'Never mind, Wils,' I say. 'I'll fill you in on the way.'

'There's something we have to get first,' she says, climbing down off the rock and into the bush again. We walk for about five minutes, keeping an ear out for the Wilders returning. Eventually, Willow stops and ducks under a low branch. She brushes dead ferns and leaves from a sheet of corrugated iron, then flips it over to expose a hole the size of a grave. There's something wrapped in a moth-eaten blanket. Willow unrolls a rifle and a box of bullets. Then she reaches into the hole again and pulls out a bow and half a dozen arrows tied together with a strip of leather. There are only ten bullets. I empty them into my pockets.

'Ready?' Willow says. She sets a course above the tree line, heading east; the morning sun is in our eyes when it pierces the canopy. She's fast—she finds gaps in the bush JT and I can't even see. Moving behind her, I notice she's grown since last year. I don't remember her being this tall, or her legs as long. Her skin is tanned a deep brown and her hair is tied in a thick ponytail with baling twine.

When she eventually stops to allow us to catch up, JT drops next to her. He's puffing, but she's hardly broken a sweat. 'How old are you?' he asks.

'Not sure,' she says. 'Maybe eleven now.'

'Eleven!' JT says.

Wils shrugs.

'We have to find water,' I say, scanning the highway below. 'We can't keep going at this pace without it.'

The wind has picked up too, a northerly bringing more heat and dust from the plains. We're already thirsty and we haven't eaten since last night.

'We've got to keep moving,' JT says. 'The Wilders will eventually work out we're not with the No-landers. And they'll guess where we're heading.'

He barely finishes before we pick up the unmistakable sound of a diesel engine. We crawl down towards the paddocks. The truck is inching its way along the highway. A second figure has climbed onto the cabin roof and they're both looking up towards us.

'Wils, do you know the country between here and Wentworth?' I ask.

'Most of it,' she says. 'The bush gets thicker. Plenty of cover but harder to travel through. There's one problem but I'll explain when we get to it.'

'What is it?

'You'll see,' she replies.

We climb a little higher towards the ridge, but not so far that we can't see the paddocks. We need to know what the Wilders are doing. The terrain's not steep and the undergrowth is dry after the long summer. But hunger and thirst are slowing us down, and the rifle I'm carrying is getting heavier by the minute. Before long we stumble across another outcrop of rocks blocking our path. Willow climbs onto the rocks and has a look around.

'Come on, Wils,' I say. 'We have to keep moving.'

'Wait,' she says, ducking between two large boulders and motioning for us to follow. There's a series of ledges protected from the sun and on one of them a shallow indent holds some of last night's rain. We take it in turns, slurping loudly as we drink. I'm the last, draining the water and sifting the mud between my teeth.

Willow sticks both her hands in the mud and smears it onto her face and arms. 'Camouflage,' she says.

The rest of the morning is a blur of sweat and scratched skin and my rumbling stomach. As Willow predicted, the forest has become thicker. It's hard to tell how much distance we've covered but at least I know every step is a step closer to Kas. Every time I feel I can't go any further, I think of her and what she must be going through.

After a couple of hours, the trees begin to thin again. We slow our pace, worried about being seen. When we edge forward we discover a valley intersecting our route east. Bare paddocks lead down to a farmhouse by a dry creek bed. A dirt road winds along the valley floor, past the house and over a rise, heading south. On the other side, there's more open ground before the safety of the trees. We can't see how far the valley stretches towards the main range.

'I'm guessing this is the problem you were talking about?' JT says to Willow.

She nods.

We sit for a few minutes, getting our breath and calculating how quickly we could make it down to the farmhouse, then up to the ridge.

'It's risky,' I say. 'But it could take us the rest of the day—or longer—to walk around. We could make it down in a couple of minutes. The climb would be slower but ten minutes max and we could be back in the trees and on our way.' In the back of my mind a little alarm bell rings—I'm making quick decisions designed to get us to Wentworth as quickly as possible, rather than focusing on staying safe. I just want to find Kas.

'I'm with you,' JT says. 'Willow?'

Willow is about to speak when we see a cloud of dust rising off the dirt road, coming from the direction of the highway. As the truck reaches the top of a small hill, the thrum of its motor overtakes the sound of the wind in the trees. It's crawling along, the lookouts still perched on the roof, the flaps billowing at the rear of the canopy. It slows further as it approaches the farmhouse, then turns through the gateway and stops in the yard. Straightaway, a dozen men spill from the back. They make a beeline for the tank and the tap is turned on. Water gushes out and they wrestle with each other to get at it. One Wilder peels off his shirt and the water sprays over his body.

It hurts to watch. My tongue sticks to the roof of my mouth, and my lips are cracked and sore.

'You reckon they know we're watching this?' JT asks.

'Fair bet,' I say. 'They always seem to be one step ahead of us.'

The cabin door on the truck opens and Tusker climbs down, carrying a rifle. He ignores the other Wilders by the tank and walks to the end of the yard. He lifts the rifle to his shoulder and, aiming somewhere to our right, shoots into the trees. He pauses before firing again, this time a little closer to our position. Two more shots, then he's aiming directly at us. We flatten ourselves to the ground as a bullet whistles over our heads. He fires another three shots away to our left.

'He knows we're here somewhere,' I say.

'But not exactly where,' JT says. 'He's trying to spook us into showing ourselves.'

'Either way,' I say, 'we'll have to climb around the valley.'

'Maybe not,' Willow says.

'Sorry, Wils,' I say. 'It's our only option.'

'No, it's not,' she says. 'What if we go the other way? Back out towards the highway—cut across the mouth of the valley.'

JT has picked up on her thinking. 'They've probably left guards at the turn-off on the highway, but there might be enough cover for us to get through between here and there.'

Willow's smart. I wouldn't have thought of this.

'At least we can check it out,' I say.

One thing goes unspoken—water. The farmhouse tank could have supplied it, but now we'll have to go without. We turn back into the trees, crawling the first few metres until we're sure we can't be seen from below. Once we get to our feet we set off at a jog, weaving through the undergrowth to find the easiest route.

13

It only takes a few minutes to reach the tree line to the north. A small rise hides us from the farmhouse. We can see as far as the intersection where the dirt road meets the highway. Sure enough, there are two men standing in the middle of the bitumen, rifles across their shoulders. The paddocks here are dry and bare of grass but there are trees dotted through them.

'One at a time or all together?' JT asks.

'One at a time,' I say, although I'm not convinced either option will work.

Willow turns and sprints for the first tree, her bow across her shoulders and the arrows in one hand. JT follows. He continues to the next tree, which has a large bough that's fallen to the ground. He slides in behind it and signals to me.

I take a last look at the Wilders on the highway, hold the rifle out in front of me and start my run. My legs are heavy—maybe from the lack of water and food, but just as likely from fear. I drop behind the tree with JT, while Willow moves further down the hill. We leapfrog each other like this until there are no trees between the highway and us. From here, we can see a concrete drain running under the dirt road. It's hard to tell how wide it is, but if we can fit through we can get to the paddock on the other side. I point it out to JT and Willow.

I can see the two Wilders better from here. They're sitting by the signpost at the intersection. Maybe the heat's getting to them, too. Sweat smears the dirt on our faces and arms.

We're about thirty metres from the drain when we hear the truck coming.

'Go!' I say, and we sprint for the side of the road.

The drain is about a metre wide but it's partially blocked with clumps of grass and dirt. I scramble in feet-first, pushing the debris ahead of me. Willow and JT crawl in behind and we wait for the truck to pass overhead. It takes forever to reach us, finally rumbling over the top of us and moving on towards the intersection.

But the sound of the motor stays within earshot. They must have stopped. We can only guess at what's happening but about five minutes pass before the truck crosses us again, retracing its route to the farmhouse.

'Maybe they changed the guards,' JT whispers.

I brace myself against the concrete walls and start kicking at the debris blocking the drain. Slowly, the sand and grass and branches give way and I see daylight. I shuffle forward but freeze when I hear voices and the sound of boots on gravel.

'You tell him,' one voice says.

'Yeah, sure,' another replies. 'Tell Tusker he's got it wrong? He'd love that. Probably shoot me for my trouble.'

'Nah, he wouldn't. Cut your balls off, maybe.'

Both men laugh.

'They'll be with the rebels by now. Way up in the main range. We're not gonna find them out there.'

'I know, but orders are orders. Come on. This'll do.'

The men drop off the side of the road and we can see the backs of their legs as they begin to walk through the paddock we've crossed. When they're out of sight I push the rifle ahead of me and squeeze through the gap at the end of the drain. Willow passes me her bow and arrows and I pull her out. Finally, JT emerges.

Men have been dropped at intervals along the road and are climbing the paddock. The truck has reached the rise and stopped. Looking the other way, I can't see any sentries at the intersection.

'Let's wait until they reach the trees and then make our run,' JT says.

Every few minutes we check on the Wilders' progress. Eventually, they reach the top of the paddock and disappear into the trees.

Ahead of us a wide stretch of open ground rises to where the canopy merges with the undergrowth. If we make it without being seen we can put some real distance between us and the Wilders.

'Ready?' I say. JT and Willow nod. Then we break cover and run.

All the way up, I'm expecting to hear shouts from across the valley, even gunshots, as the Wilders spot us. We stick close together, in case one of us falls or needs help. Adrenaline kicks in and gets even the most tired muscles pumping.

By some miracle, we make it to the trees without being seen. We plunge into the bracken and collapse onto our hands and knees. JT is panting heavily and Willow dry retches. I roll onto my back and try to focus, but everything is spinning.

It takes a while to recover but when we've got our breath we crawl to where we can see into the valley. The truck is turning around and the Wilders haven't reappeared from the forest on the opposite ridge. The hot wind whips the trees above our heads and lifts dust off the dirt road in great whirlwinds.

We're exhausted but we'll have to get going soon. JT and I have lain down again, trying to get some energy back into our bodies.

'Oh no!' Willow says suddenly.

We jump up and look across the valley. The Wilders have broken from the trees in one big group. Running. At the front, one of them holds a dog that's straining at its lead, pulling him down the hill. It's Rowdy. He follows our scent, tree by tree, sniffing and jumping around each fallen log before continuing to the next one. When they get to the drain under the road, the

Wilder lets Rowdy off the lead. He bolts through and heads straight for us.

JT grabs the rifle out of my hands, slides the bolt and takes aim. I throw myself at him before he can shoot. 'No! It's Rowdy, it's Rowdy.'

'He's leading them straight to us,' JT yells above the wind. We struggle over the rifle, rolling on top of each other now, with Willow trying to pull us apart.

Rowdy lunges into the brush and jumps onto us. He's so excited, barking, then licking my face. He recognises Willow and does the same to her. In the confusion I manage to prise the rifle out of JT's hands. He gets to his feet and backs away.

'What were you thinking?' I scream. His face is red and he clenches his fists like he's ready for a fight.

'Jesus, Finn—look!' he says, pointing down the hill.

The Wilders have climbed onto the road above the pipe, where the truck now waits. Tusker gathers them together, his arms waving, issuing orders again. Half of them get into the truck, while the rest drop off the bank and run towards us. Tusker climbs back into the cabin, drives to the intersection and turns right, in the direction of Wentworth.

JT's in my face. 'Your dog's gonna get us killed,' he snaps.

'But—'

Willow steps between us. 'Come on,' she says. 'We've gotta move. Now!'

JT reels away, shaking his head and mumbling under his breath.

'Which way?' I say, slinging the rifle over my shoulder.

'They must have guessed we're heading for Wentworth,' Willow says. 'We could confuse them by backtracking.' She points up the valley towards the farmhouse.

There's no time to argue. We start running parallel to the dirt road, far enough into the trees not to be seen from below. We stick together, Rowdy at my heels.

As we get closer to the farmhouse, our pace slows. Adrenaline can only keep us up for so long. Every hot intake of breath burns my lungs. The image of the Wilders standing underneath the water tank keeps flashing into my head. I can almost taste the cool water pouring into my mouth, splashing my face.

Willow stumbles over a log. I stop and reach down for her but she shrugs my hand away and gets to her feet. Rowdy's tongue lolls out the side of his mouth and he pants heavily.

'Let's hope we've outsmarted them,' I manage to say. 'Cos I don't think we can outrun them.'

The farmhouse is directly below us now. It looks abandoned again. We peer back through the trees, trying to pick up the sound of the Wilders above the roaring of the wind.

'I think we should split up,' JT says.

'We don't have time for this, JT,' I say, knowing he's still angry with me. 'We promised to stick together.'

'That was before Rowdy gave us away,' he says. 'You're too blind to see it, but we need to get rid of him.' He nods his head towards the gun.

'No way,' I say. 'Never!'

Rowdy hides behind my legs, like he knows he's in trouble.

Willow stands with her feet apart and hands on hips. 'Cut

it out,' she says. 'You're being stupid. They'd hear the shot.'

JT can't look me in the eye. He scuffs at the ground with his boot.

'We're all in this together,' Willow says, sounding final.

There's a large wattle that's been uprooted completely and its branches form a shelter close to the ground. We crawl inside and wait. I've got Rowdy by the collar and I tap his nose like I did so many times when we were hunting in Angowrie. I want to hold him and breathe in his familiar smell.

I guess it's about fifteen minutes before we venture out again. If the Wilders knew which way we'd come, they would've been on us by now. We've bought ourselves some time, though who knows how long it'll be before they work out we've backtracked.

'What now?' Willow asks.

'We can't go any further without water,' I say. 'I reckon we go down to the farmhouse.'

Willow and JT look at me like I'm crazy. And, to be honest, I don't know if I am or not. The lack of food and water makes it hard to think straight. JT stands up and walks to the edge of the bush. He looks up and down the valley, weighing our chances of getting to the house and back without being caught.

'Okay,' he says. 'But one of us needs to go first. If it's a trap, the other two have the option of running.'

'It's my idea,' I say. 'I'll go. Wils, hang onto Rowdy so he doesn't follow me.' I think about handing the rifle to JT, but change my mind.

Willow pins me with her gaze. 'Be careful.'

I pat Rowdy and pass him to Willow, who holds him by the

collar. I take a deep breath, check the road one more time—and run. My eyes are fixed on the house rather than on what's under my feet and the ground is steep. I nearly fall half a dozen times and the rifle butt slaps against my hip. But I make it to the road without hearing any shouting or being shot at. I slide into a ditch, gasping for air. After I've settled myself, I crawl up the embankment, check the road and sprint for the side of the house. I peer through a broken window. There's bedding on the floor and empty cans strewn around. At the rear, a door hangs by one hinge, creaking in the wind.

I do a quick check, then signal to JT and Willow. At the tank stand I reach up, turn the tap and the coolest, sweetest water I have ever tasted pours into my mouth. I let the water shower over me. I gulp at it, snorting like a horse. When I've had enough, I peer around the corner towards the road.

Willow comes next, racing through the dry stubble of the paddock. Rowdy bounds ahead of her and reaches me before she's halfway down. She doesn't stop at the road, coming straight across, passing me and heading for the tank. Once she's made it, JT leaves the safety of the trees.

Willow is standing under the flowing water, her face turned up to meet it. 'Oh, my god,' she says, over and over. 'This is so good.'

JT arrives, drops his gear and nudges in beside her. The wind whips the spray sideways and they jump about to catch it.

I push open the door to the house. It has a lived-in smell. There are dishes in the sink and knives and forks on the bench. I find a bowl and walk back out to the yard. JT and Willow are soaked. They've found some plastic bottles and they're filling them. Once they're done I hold the bowl for Rowdy. He laps at it until it's empty—then I fill it up again.

'I don't like it here,' I say. 'There's been someone living in the house.'

Wils and JT go in to have a look. 'Hey.' JT's voice rises above the wind.

When I come inside he's standing in front of an open cupboard. The shelves are almost bare but there are three cans without labels and a stack that looks like sardines. Willow has found a small daypack. The straps have rotted away but there's a loop at the top that's still attached. We throw the cans in, looking around the kitchen for anything else. We take a can opener, a kitchen knife and two spoons. Then we force the water bottles into the pack with them, and run out into the yard.

'One more thing,' Willow says. She walks to the tank and turns the tap on, leaving it running. 'Now they can be thirsty, too.'

We cross the road, barely bothering to stop and look, and begin the climb. By the time we get to the trees, our clothes are dry and we're nearly as thirsty as we were fifteen minutes ago.

We crawl under the fallen tree. Willow spreads the cans out on the ground. The sardines have ring-pulls and we peel two lids back and have a sniff. They're oily and salty, but we're so hungry we don't care. When I offer a couple to Rowdy he wolfs them down.

JT opens one of the bigger cans. 'Shit and preservatives, anyone?' he says, sounding more like the JT I know.

It's some sort of stew or thick soup but we pass it around. It's sticky and glutinous and probably way out of date, but I don't think I've ever tasted anything as good.

Willow hands around a water bottle. 'Just a few sips,' she says. 'We have to make it last.' Every time she says something like this, something adult and sensible, I hear Stella's voice.

'What?' she says, seeing me looking.

'Nothing, Wils. Good thinking, that's all. Rationing the water, I mean.'

She smiles.

My stomach is nowhere near full, but it feels so much better to have something in it. I can't stop burping.

'You've got fish breath,' Willow says, forcing up a burp herself.

JT has stuck his head outside. 'Shh,' he says.

All I can hear is the wind roaring through the branches above us but JT climbs back in, shoves the remaining cans into the pack. 'Come on,' he says.

We gather our gear and crawl out. JT is already running further up the hill, so Willow and I follow. Rowdy is ahead with JT.

'Wait,' I call. The last thing we need now is to get lost. We catch up to JT, each of us breathing hard again. 'What did you hear?' I ask.

'The truck. Heading for the house,' he says, his breath coming in gasps. 'They'll know we've been there.'

'Shit,' I say.

'Shit,' Willow agrees.

'Which way do you reckon?' JT asks.

It seems my life since the virus has been a string of quick decisions. I never know whether they're right or wrong until things either go pear-shaped or they don't. Mostly they're guesses. But I'm getting better at making them.

'Our best chance of making it to Wentworth is to follow the highway—or at least to keep it in sight,' I say.

I'm sure we're all thinking the same thing. We could walk straight into the Wilders if they've figured out what we've done. And why was the truck heading back to the farmhouse if they think we're moving east?

JT has been listening carefully, his head turning one way then the other, calculating the odds. 'Okay,' he says, finally. 'But we need to go higher. If they're coming back to meet the truck, they'll most likely be in the open where the going's easier. Let's climb to the top, keep the sun at our left shoulder and see how far we get.'

The ground is stonier and less stable here but we feel safer the higher we go. Eventually we spy another rock outcrop above the treetops. We drop our gear at its base and circle around to find the easiest way up. We can see the plains in the distance and the power poles along the railway line but the trees block any view of the farmhouse. At least we can orientate ourselves now. The wind has finally backed off a bit, though it's still hard to hear anything above it.

We continue for about an hour, getting slower the further we go. Finally, JT calls a rest and we slump into the bracken. Rowdy lies next to me. He's panting hard and licking my skin looking for moisture. I tip a little water into my hand, and he laps it up. I feel like JT is judging my every action. He watches closely, knowing every drop Rowdy has is less for us.

'I'm stuffed,' JT says, eventually. 'Let's rest here for a while and move on when it's cooler.'

He gets no argument from Willow or me. We make ourselves as comfortable as we can on the rough ground and doze. Rowdy nuzzles at the scar on his hip. When I scratch him under his chin he closes his eyes and groans quietly. I've lost him so many times over the past year but somehow we manage to find each other again. And now, even though he's safe, I still feel I need to keep him close.

I must have slept because the sun is slanting low through the trees when Willow gives me a nudge. JT is standing on a log, trying to get his bearings. 'How far do you reckon we've come from the farmhouse?' he asks.

'It's been pretty rough going but I'd guess two k's,' Willow replies.

'Yeah, I'm thinking the same,' JT says.

'So?' I ask.

JT moves his head from side to side. 'Maybe we should head north while we've got the sun to navigate by—get a bit lower where we can see the highway again. If the Wilders have back-tracked, they'll be in the valley we crossed by now. Besides,' he says, sweeping an arm to take in the bush surrounding us, 'we'll never make it to Wentworth struggling through this country.'

The heat has finally started to leave the forest and the wind has dropped to a breeze as we start to pick our way downhill. It takes longer than we'd expected, and the sun is dipping behind the ridges to the west when the paddocks come into view. We stop for a minute, peering through the trees and listening for any sign of danger. When we're confident it's okay, we keep moving, slower now, with me gripping Rowdy by the collar.

The last trees are low-slung stringybarks, like the ones down on the coast. We edge forward until we can take in the whole scene in front of us. The glow from the setting sun catches the surface of dams dotted over the plains, lighting them like tiny sheets of gold. Closer to us, the highway stretches out—the flat asphalt rising above the stubble and bare ground. Next to it, the railway tracks head west to Longley, east to Wentworth.

'What's that?' Willow says, pointing to where a dirt road coming in off the plain meets the highway. The sun catches something large and metallic by the side of the road.

'A sign, maybe?' I say.

'And what do road signs say?' JT asks.

'Distance to the next town,' Willow says.

We know we need a plan to rescue Kas and Daymu, but we have to know where we are and how far we've got to travel.

'It'll be dark in half an hour,' JT says. 'Let's wait, then go down and check it out.'

It's the perfect spot to watch the night fall on the plain. We look for any sign of movement along the highway or through the paddocks but everything is still and calm after the heat of the day. Rabbits move out into the open to nibble at the patchy grass. They don't worry about us, coming within a few metres of where we're sitting. Rowdy twitches beside me, ready to spring. Moving almost in slow motion, Willow eases an arrow into her bow. She raises it to her shoulder, pulls the arrow back, then releases. A rabbit scuttles sideways, trying to find its feet again, the arrow piercing its side. Willow is on it in an instant, grabbing it by the back legs and quickly stretching its neck. She retrieves her arrow then throws the rabbit to Rowdy. 'Here you go, boy. We can't risk a fire, but you're probably not fussed about eating it raw.'

Rowdy drags the carcass back into the bush and tears at the flesh.

JT looks on, his eyes wide.

'I told you,' I say, feeling like I need to get back on even terms with him. 'Don't cross Willow. She'll put an arrow in you!'

Once it's fully dark, we cross the paddock to the highway. Rowdy carries a bloodied hindquarter of the rabbit in his mouth. There's a rusty wire fence, then an embankment leading up to the road. We stay in its shadow and walk towards the sign. One of the timber legs has sagged into the soil and the writing is faded but we can make it out.

Wentworth 37 km.

14

'We can walk that in two days,' I say, 'if we don't have any hold-ups.'

'We're here now,' JT adds. 'We should stay on the road—at least until the moon rises.'

It seems stupid to expose ourselves like this, but we can make good distance, and walking in the open is the last thing the Wilders will expect us to do.

After the long day in the sun, the cool of the night is a relief. But my lips are cracked and blistered and I've got a lump in my throat that feels like the sardines have stuck there. It must be fourteen hours since we took off from the No-landers' camp.

My body aches from the endless running and walking, and I'm constantly on edge knowing that Tusker won't rest until he finds us.

The road goes straight for a while before curving to the left and crossing the railway line. After another hour, there's a faint glow on the horizon and the moon appears above the hills to the east. It's bigger again than last night, strong enough to cast shadows once it gets up. It makes us feel more exposed, with nothing but flat paddocks either side of the road. We quicken our pace.

JT has been walking ahead of us but now he waits for Willow and me to catch up. 'Look,' he says, pointing to a building about a hundred metres along the road. The shell of a petrol station takes shape in the shadows of a row of manna gums. A fallen sign marks the entrance, surrounded by knee-high weeds, and nearer to the building, two bowsers stand like sentries, their hoses ripped out and lying on the ground.

We push through the front door, the crunch of broken glass under our feet. Tables line one wall and there's a servery opening to a kitchen at the back. I stick my head through. There's an oven, a sink, a deep fryer and the sharp smell of rancid cooking oil.

Out the back, a ute sits on its chassis, its wheels long gone.

JT finds a broom and sweeps out a storeroom. We lie down and try to get comfortable.

'We should keep watch,' I say. 'I'll go first.'

I take a chair out the front, positioning it next to one of the bowsers. Rowdy lies across my feet and I prop the rifle against my thigh. I'm exhausted but anxious enough to stay awake. Compared to the forest, there's not much noise out here, the occasional hoot of an owl and the scrambling of rats in the rubbish heaped at the side of the main building.

I wonder who made a living out of this place before the virus. Maybe farmers dropped in for a coffee and newspapers, talking beef prices and the cost of fertiliser. Long-haul truckers pulling in for a feed in the early morning—bacon and eggs, sausages and baked beans on toast. My mouth waters at the thought. There would have been a constant stream of traffic on the highway: holidaymakers hauling caravans down towards Nelson and the west coast, local boys in hotted-up utes drag-racing their mates to Longley for the night, families taking a toilet break while mum or dad filled up with petrol and washed the windscreen. Something in my heart aches for the everyday things we've lost.

I may have dozed for a while but Rowdy brings me back. He's standing to attention, his coat bristling and his nose pointed along the road towards Longley. He growls low and long.

I grab the rifle and walk towards the road. It's perfectly still now, not a breath of wind and the moon is high and as bright as it's been all night. The sound begins as a faint whirring but it quickly gathers strength to become a low rumble. It's a truck.

I race back inside and wake the others. We scramble to gather our gear then take cover in the kitchen. There's a door heading out the back to the workshop but we're out of time—the truck is almost on us. JT clears the shelves under the stainless steel servery bench, sweeping pots and pans out onto the floor until there's enough space to crawl into.

The truck slows, revving as it changes down gears.

It's stopping.

The bulk of the truck fills the whole space at the front of the station, darkening the kitchen. The driver cuts the engine and it's quiet enough to hear the motor ping and click as it begins to cool.

I squeeze Rowdy between me and the wall and hold my hand over his muzzle. I scratch him behind his ear to calm him. Boots drop onto the concrete and there's the sound of piss hitting the ground.

A voice I know barks, 'Check it out. One inside, one around the back.' It's Tusker.

Cautious footsteps approach. Someone leans through the servery window and the bench groans under their weight.

'Anything?' I hear Tusker ask.

There's a short hesitation, then, 'Why are we even looking here? Their trackers are active. They're in Wentworth.'

'Someone had been at the house, stealing food. And the water was left running.'

'It could have been rebels.'

Rowdy starts to fidget and I bury my face in his coat to reassure him.

'I don't trust the trackers,' Tusker says, his voice low and menacing. 'And that dog was on the scent of something.'

'Could've been a rabbit. Could've been anything.'

Tusker snorts. 'They're kids—they'll make a mistake eventually. We'll patrol the road. And anyway, if they try to get to

Wentworth, they'll never get through the fences.'

Tusker's voice trails off as he moves out the front, but the other Wilder stays where he is. Then, he walks through the door into the kitchen. He doesn't have a torch so it's only the moonlight coming through the window that allows him to see anything at all—shadows and a jumble of cooking gear spread across the floor. He pauses, listening and sniffing the air. I hadn't even thought of what we must smell like, how that might give us away. I hope the stench of rancid cooking oil blankets our scent.

'All right, let's go,' Tusker calls from outside.

The man in the kitchen stays. He's so close I could reach out and touch his leg. Finally, he walks slowly out, his footfalls soft, as though he's still listening.

The truck engine comes to life and diesel fumes waft into the kitchen. It moves off slowly, heading towards Wentworth.

'Woah!' JT says as the motor fades into the distance. 'That was close.'

Willow exhales hard, as though she's been holding her breath. Rowdy pushes past me and stretches once he's on the floor.

'You heard what Tusker said,' I say. 'They're going to patrol the highway.'

'There's no way we're going to be on the road during the day,' JT says. 'But we can hear them coming at night. It gives us a chance to hide.'

'We were lucky,' I say. 'If they'd come earlier we'd have been caught in the open.'

'Everything's a risk, Finn. It's a risk having Rowdy with us.' There's an edge to his voice again. He hasn't let go of our fight this afternoon.

'What did he mean by the fences?' Willow asks, cutting off another potential argument over Rowdy.

'No idea,' I say.

'So…?' Willow asks.

'We keep moving,' JT says. 'Look for somewhere off the road before daybreak. There'll be old farmhouses out here.' I know the thought of Daymu being held captive is driving him in the same way Kas is driving me. All of our decisions are mixed up with the desperate need to get to Wentworth. And we haven't even begun to think about how we'll find them once we get there.

The only gauge of time is the arcing of the moon. It's behind us now and our shadows lengthen as we strike out onto the highway again. We're slower—the lack of sleep and food catching up with us. Willow never complains. Every time I look at her, she nods, puts her head down, and keeps going.

As the night wears on, our rest breaks become longer and it's harder to get going again. There have been no patrols, and eventually the sky in the east begins to lighten. Off to our left, maybe two hundred metres away, I spy a hayshed with a windmill and water tank. We can't get to it fast enough, stumbling across the paddocks towards the shed. It's collapsed on one side but there's some protection from the road. The tank is rusted out and empty but we still have two water bottles from the farmhouse. There's no hay in the shed but there are some hessian sacks in one corner. They stink of rat shit, but we lie on them anyway.

Once the sun comes up, the temperature inside the shed rises quickly—it's going to be another scorcher. Before we try to sleep, we open another can—vegetable stew this time—and share it around. Rowdy isn't interested—he ate all the rabbit Willow shot. We drink the second-last bottle of water.

Three times during the long, hot day, trucks thunder past on the highway—two heading towards Longley and one to Wentworth. We doze on and off, waking every time the wind lifts loose sheets of iron on the roof. The whole shed bangs and clatters and creaks. It feels like it could collapse on us at any moment.

We're awake by late afternoon, impatient for the sun to set. The wind has howled all day and the corrugated iron walls have concentrated the heat. We're sweaty and hungry and we've nearly finished the last of the water. When we step out of the shed in the evening, there are thick black clouds rising off the horizon to the west. It's both a relief and a worry when we see them. We'll struggle to walk through a storm but at least there'll be water to drink.

Once it's fully dark, we cross the paddock to the highway and continue on our way. The next road sign tells us we're within twenty k's of Wentworth. It spurs us on and we make good time, the storm looming at our backs with lightning streaking the sky and thunder rumbling every few minutes. Rowdy whines and stays close to my leg. He hates storms.

The rain arrives quickly, progressing from steady drops to

a total downpour in half a minute. There are deep puddles in potholes on the road. We stop to fill our bottles and drink, lying on our stomachs and sucking at the cleaner water on top. We trudge on, cringing when the thunder is close enough to shake the ground. Up ahead, JT waves us to the side of the road. There's a bridge over a creek. We slide down the bank and climb in underneath. It's not comfortable but it's dry and we're out of sight. The rain cascades off the side of the bridge, and the creek runs with muddy water, carrying weeds and debris with it.

Within twenty minutes the rain eases and the wind drops. The bank below the road is a slick of mud, and we have to help each other up. But, before long, we're moving again, the storm ahead of us now, the lightning cracking horizontally across the blackened sky.

We've seen no trucks during the night. Towards morning, five or six hours on from the bridge, the clouds clear completely and the stars fan out across the sky. There are more buildings in clusters now, sheds and farmhouses with windmills turning in the breeze. It feels like we're getting closer to civilisation. Just before dawn, the road rises to a small crest. We approach it warily, not knowing what lies beyond. There's a stonewall at right angles to the road, crumbled and ruined in parts but still standing in others. We turn off and follow it, staying low and finally unloading our gear. We peer over the top.

We cannot believe what we see.

15

Beyond the rise a long, ragged wall stretches across the plain, cutting off the highway. It's made of car bodies, rusted machinery, logs, a bus, railway sleepers, roofing iron, telephone poles lying at skewed angles, scrap metal, lumps of concrete and hundreds of car tyres.

On the road, there's a checkpoint with a boom gate painted red and white. There's a sentry box and armed guards in uniform.

'This must be what Tusker meant by the fences,' JT says, trying to take in what he's seeing.

Fifty metres to our right, there's a building made of the same stone as the wall. Before it gets too light, we make our way to it. It looks like it's a hundred years old. The four walls are standing, but there are no doors or windows, or roof. At one end there is a fireplace and the remains of a chimney.

'This'll have to do,' JT says. 'I don't think we can be seen from the road. We can sleep here, and tonight we'll check out the fence.'

'Tusker said *fences*. Plural. How many can there be?' I say.

'Who knows?' JT says. 'But we've come this far. We've gotta find a way through.'

The day isn't as hot as the last two. High clouds have followed the storm and they block some of the sun's intensity, though the air's thick with humidity. We sit the bottles on the floor and allow the sediment to settle. The water is still murky, but we don't have any choice. We need fluids.

I'm getting used to sleeping rough again. I find a spot in the lee of the northern wall to lie down. Rowdy sniffs his way around, pissing in half a dozen places to mark his territory, then settles inside the doorway. Willow is further along from me and JT is propped up near the fireplace. We've made it this far without being captured but the fence has spooked us. Who are they defending the city from? Or who are they trying to stop from escaping?

We sleep on and off through the day. There are more trucks on the road than yesterday, mostly heading towards Longley. Early in the afternoon, two army vehicles speed past, moving west.

Later, I pick up a strange buzzing noise coming from the

direction of the fence. It gets louder for a while then fades. JT and Willow have heard it too. We keep to the back of the house then make the short run to the stone wall. The fence looks even more bizarre in the full light of day. It's like someone has emptied a rubbish tip and piled it up in a row. For the first time, we see the heavy coils of razor wire laced through it, and we pick up the stench of it too—something is rotting in among the tyres, concrete and steel.

Slowly, the buzzing noise draws closer. A drone skims through the air above the fence. It stops, hovers and turns towards us. We drop behind the stone wall and lie along its base. I try to hold Rowdy by the collar but the buzzing is almost over us now and he starts barking. He wrenches free and tears into the open, running in circles as the drone hovers above him. It stays for a few seconds, turning one way then the other, before moving towards the house. Rowdy chases it, leaping in the air and yapping wildly.

It comes back our way but veers off to the highway and follows the road to the gate. It hovers there for a short while then resumes its surveillance of the fence, heading north.

With the drone gone, Rowdy settles and joins us.

JT is fuming. 'I told you,' he says, between gritted teeth. 'That dog's gonna get us killed. Now we have to move in the daylight. We'll be sitting ducks.'

'He couldn't help it,' I say, knowing it sounds pathetic.

'He couldn't, but *we* could,' JT fires back. 'We should've got rid of him at the farmhouse.'

Rowdy hides behind my legs.

Willow steps between JT and me. 'Do you think they saw us?' she asks.

'They definitely saw Rowdy,' JT says.

'How much more daylight do you reckon we've got?' Willow asks.

'Two, maybe three hours,' I guess.

JT is still seething as we gather our gear and make our way back to the wall. Heading away from the road, it follows a rocky ridge before it peters out near a small clump of trees that might give us some cover.

We keep as low as we can, sprinting harder where there are gaps in the wall. The last stretch to the trees is completely open. We hesitate for a few seconds before JT says, 'Go!'

There are only half a dozen trees in the clump, surrounded by stumps where others have been cut and hauled away. The remaining ones are twisted and gnarled, with thin strips of bark hanging off them. When I look up into the branches, something catches my eye. Where two trees lean into each other there's a platform screened by foliage. I give Rowdy the signal to stay and he drops. There are notches cut in the trunk for footholds and, a little higher up, a knotted rope. We start to climb—me first, then Willow and JT. The platform is made of wide, flat boards nailed to the branches. It's bare except for an empty binoculars case.

When I part the branches we have a perfect line of sight down to the sentry post on the highway.

'Someone's been using this to keep an eye on the fence,' JT says.

'But who?' Willow asks.

'Maybe people wanting to get in,' I say. 'Like us.'

'Or someone watching traffic on the road,' JT says. 'Like No-landers.'

'Either way, we'll have to stay here until it gets dark,' I say.

The afternoon drags. There's not enough room for us to stretch out on the planks. I climb down a couple of times to reassure Rowdy. Finally, the sun dips in the west and the day begins to melt into the evening.

We're just starting to relax when Willow whispers. 'We got trouble!'

I shuffle up next to her and look where she's pointing. There's a group of soldiers making their way—no, running—towards the sentry post from the Wentworth side. The boom gate opens and they pass straight through, veer off the road and make a beeline for the stone house.

'Shit!' JT says. 'What do we do?'

The soldiers are almost at the stone wall, their figures hazy in the dusk.

'We can't stay here,' I say. 'They'll see the trees from the house and come to investigate.'

We climb down, keeping the trunk between the soldiers and us. We hit the ground running, past the last few trees then over a small ridge and downhill to the fence. From there, we take off away from the sentry post. The fence curves away to the south, giving us some protection.

Up close the fence is much higher than it seemed from a distance—a crazy jumble of sharp metal and broken concrete that towers over us. We look desperately for footholds but there's razor wire coiled through the stack. We couldn't get over without being cut to shreds. We keep running, becoming more frantic the longer we go. It's getting darker by the minute, so at least that works in our favour.

A whistle pierces the air and men shout to each other. Above the panic and confusion I hear a loud popping sound and everything is suddenly flooded with light. It's then we see the cable, looping from pole to pole along the top of the fence and, at regular intervals, long fluorescent tubes hanging by their wires.

We run blindly along the fence. There's the crack of gunfire and the sound of bullets hitting metal. Willow's breath is loud, Rowdy has started to bark and JT is trying to run and load the rifle at the same time. Up ahead the hulking shape of a bus sticks out from the fence, blocking our path. We run to the other side and look for somewhere to hide. As we stand in its shadow, dark figures jump out through the windows and doors, landing on us, punching and kicking. I feel an arm wrap itself around my mouth and I'm dragged inside the bus, vaguely aware—through the blur of boots and fists—of JT and Willow being pulled in behind me. Rowdy leaps into the fray but a kick knocks him sideways and he cringes under one of the seats. The door is pulled shut and everything is quiet apart from the heavy breathing of our attackers and us.

'Any noise and I'll slit your throat,' a voice whispers in my ear. I feel a cold blade against my throat.

Boots approach, pause for a few seconds then continue past the bus. A minute passes and two hands grab me by the shirt and haul me off the floor. The light filters into the bus and I see Willow and JT being lifted in the same way. There are four dark figures all with rags tied across their faces so only their eyes are showing.

The one holding me speaks first. 'Who are you?' he demands. It's a boy's voice.

'Nobody,' I say, still struggling to find my breath.

'What? I can't understand you,' he says.

I do my best to slow down and speak clearly. 'We're on the run,' I say.

'From who?'

'Wilders. The army.'

'Why?'

'We escaped from a transport. Back towards Longley.' I'm hyperventilating. It hardly sounds like me talking.

'Why are you here?'

'We're trying to get to Wentworth.'

Now the others laugh. 'Bullshit!' one of them says.

Another figure peers out the back window. 'Clear,' he says.

Willow and JT are shoved in next to me and we're lined up on a bench seat. Our attackers stand over us.

'They're Sileys,' the boy says, pointing to the lump on the back of my hand.

'Not this one.' I'm surprised to hear a girl's voice. She's holding Willow's arm.

'They don't look like Sileys,' one of the others says. He sounds even younger.

'We were reclassified,' JT says. 'In Longley.'

'So it's true. We heard rumours about that,' the girl says.

'You know Ramage?' JT asks. 'He's commissioner of the zone west of here.'

'Yes, we know him. How long have you been running?' the girl asks.

'Our transport was attacked a couple of days ago,' I say.

'By who?'

'No-landers.'

'You've met the rebels?' the boy says, excited now.

'And who are you?' JT asks.

The girl nods to each of them and they slowly unwind the rags around their faces. There are two boys and two girls. The girls and one of the boys are dark-skinned. The second boy is blond-haired, tall and thin.

'Survivors,' the tall boy says. 'I'm Tamas and this is Ash,' he says pointing to the other boy. 'And Sarisi and Vidu.' The girls each raise a hand.

I tell them our names.

'Are you Sileys?' Willow asks.

'Not any more,' Sarisi says. She holds up her hand. It has a scar across the back, a couple of centimetres long.

'And you?' Willow says, nodding at Tamas.

'Freeborn,' Tamas says. 'But that doesn't mean much these days.'

I look more closely at Sarisi's scar. 'That's dangerous,' I say. 'I know someone who died doing that.'

'We have our connections,' she says. 'It was done properly.' She pauses for a second. 'But you two, you're on the grid.'

JT smiles and shakes his head. 'What?' Sarisi says.

'Long story,' JT says. 'But we're not on the grid. Our trackers aren't active. I guarantee it.'

'You can deactivate them?'

'Yeah,' JT says with a sideways glance at me.

Now that they've sorted out who we are, they're not sure what to do with us.

'Why did you help us?' I ask.

'We've been watching you—at the stone house and in the lookout tree,' Ash says. His hair is roughly cut, almost to his scalp. There's something familiar about him but I can't put my finger on it.

'Do you live inside the fences?' JT asks.

A look passes around the group. Sarisi seems to be the leader. 'Why is that important?' she says.

'We need to get in.'

Again, they laugh.

'You have no idea, do you?' Tamas says. 'It's dangerous in there. There are patrols—and drones, as you've already discovered.'

Vidu has coaxed Rowdy out from under the seat. She pats him with soft strokes along his back.

'Can you get us through the fences?' I ask.

Sarisi puffs her cheeks and exhales. 'No,' she says firmly. 'Go home. If you are captured inside the city you'll be slaves for life.'

'There are people we need to find,' JT says.

Sarisi nods. 'We all have friends and family in there,' she says. 'But the virus is still active, so everything is monitored.'

'We just need to get in,' JT says. 'We'll take our chances.'

'You think you're brave,' Ash says. 'But you're stupid. You can survive outside the fences. Find a quarantined town. Lie low.'

I snort and they all look at me. 'What do you think I've been doing for three winters?' I say. 'It's not safe out there either.'

'Who is it you're looking for?' Tamas asks.

JT hesitates, looking to me, then Willow. 'Two girls, Sileys,' he says.

'You've got no chance,' Ash replies. 'The women are kept in a separate part of the city. A whole block fenced off and guarded.'

'So?' JT says, scratching his head. 'Are the fences designed to keep people in or out?'

'Both,' Sarisi says.

'But you can get us in,' he says again. This conversation is going in circles.

'If there was a purpose to it, yes, we could get you in,' Sarisi says, growing more agitated. 'But we don't know these Sileys. They are nobody to us.'

'What if we try to get in ourselves?' JT says. 'It must be possible.'

Sarisi shakes her head. 'You'd be captured before you got to the second fence. You can stay here until the lights go out, then you must leave. The way you came.'

'When do the lights go out?' I ask.

Sarisi is wearing a watch. She looks at it now. 'In a couple of hours,' she says.

'You have time,' I say. 'A watch.'

She shrugs her shoulders. 'It helps to know when they'll have power and when they won't,' she explains. 'Two and a half hours every night—eight till ten-thirty. That's when the lights come on and the factories start up.'

'You might as well get comfortable,' Ash says.

JT, Willow and I move to the back of the bus. Rowdy has made a new friend in Vidu. He loves the attention.

We keep our voices low. 'I'm not giving up on Kas,' I say.

'Or Daymu,' JT says, a little too loudly. The others come towards us, forming a half circle, blocking the light.

'What did you say?' Ash demands.

'We said we're not giving up on our friends,' JT replies.

'The names you used—what were they?'

'Kas and Daymu,' I say.

Ash drops to his knees and stares at me. 'Daymu,' he says. 'Describe her.'

'Short, straight dark hair, light brown skin. She's Burmese.'

'Karen,' Ash corrects me.

'Yeah, that's right.'

The others huddle around Ash. His body begins to shake.

I look at him closely now, the eyes, the high cheekbones. 'You're her brother!' I say.

His eyes gleam. 'Her twin,' he says.

16

The lights go out just as Sarisi predicted. She and Ash have agreed to guide us into the city. The others will return to their base somewhere in the bush between here and the coast. JT and I try to convince Willow she should go with them but she won't be persuaded. She's sticking with us.

Sarisi refuses to take Rowdy. 'You saw how he reacted to the drone,' she says. 'There'll be more of them inside the fences. He'll give us away for sure.'

JT flashes me a look that says *I told you so*.

'Don't worry,' Vidu says. 'I'll look after him.'

Having only just found him again, it rips my heart out to

leave him behind. 'Sorry, boy,' I say, giving him a hug. 'I'll come back and get you, I promise.' Rowdy pushes his face into my chest. He knows I'm leaving.

We're given dark scarves to cover our faces—not only to stay hidden, but to protect us from infection.

We begin by climbing through the shattered front windscreen of the bus, which leads to a network of tunnels among the debris. JT struggles with the rifle and Willow has to pass her bow and arrows through to me half a dozen times. There are animals in here—rats and lizards and, Ash tells us, snakes that like to hunt at night. And there's the constant reek of something rotting. I don't want to ask what it might be.

At times, we're crawling on our bellies through dirt and mud—at others, climbing higher in the pile near the razor wire. Our bodies are cut and scratched. Eventually, we come out on top of a shipping container with a rope dropping into the no-man's-land that separates us from the next fence.

'This is as close as we can get,' Sarisi whispers. 'It's three hundred metres across. Aim for the pile of bricks. You'll know it when you see it. We go one at a time.' She nods to Ash and he shimmies down the rope and zigzags through the open field, his head low and his legs pumping.

'You next,' she says to JT. He follows Ash's route but stumbles and falls before he gets halfway. Somehow, he keeps his momentum, rolling forward and planting his feet under himself again.

'Maybe Wils and I should go together,' I say. Willow has been hanging onto my arm. Her hand is hot and sweaty.

'Okay,' Sarisi says. 'Go!'

Willow slips down the rope easily and I follow close behind. We start our run towards the vague outline of the second fence. The ground has been ploughed recently and it's boggy after last night's rain. Claggy mud clings to our boots, but slowly the fence becomes more distinct and I see JT crouching by a pile of bricks.

Sarisi almost beats us there. She moves so quickly I get a fright when she sprints up next to us.

The second fence is higher and wider than the first, but there are no lights. Again, we follow a maze of tunnels and gaps, avoiding the razor wire, until we're through to the other side.

I'm ready to run again when Ash grabs me by the shirt. 'Not here,' he says. 'There are booby traps.' He leads us further along the wall, until we come to a creek. We slide down into the reeds lining the bank. He steps into the water and immediately sinks to his waist. We follow. The water is up to Willow's chest and she gasps with the cold.

We wade forward, every so often being forced to dive under where coiled wire crosses the creek. The water stinks of sewage and there's plastic and rubbish everywhere. The scarves over our mouths protect us from the worst of it but I'm careful to block my nose and keep my eyes shut tight when we go under.

Up ahead, a huge pipe comes into view and eventually we crawl onto a concrete chute and into its gaping mouth.

'Don't worry,' Sarisi says, smiling. 'It's just stormwater.'

'Doesn't smell like it,' JT says, retching.

Willow is shivering and I rub the sides of her arms to try

to warm her. She allows me to do it for a few seconds, then moves away and pulls the bow over her shoulder.

It's easier going inside the pipe—the water is only ankle deep, though the smell is more concentrated. Sarisi has a torch to light the way. We run, the sound of our splashing boots echoing ahead of us. We come to a number of intersections with other pipes—some smaller, some as large—but Sarisi doesn't hesitate. After about twenty minutes of hard going, she slows. 'Not much further,' she says.

A metal ladder appears in the torch beam. Sarisi nods, and Ash starts climbing. Willow is next, then me, JT and, finally, Sarisi. My boots are soaked and I struggle for grip on the metal rungs. I nearly fall a couple of times but JT steadies me from below.

We enter an access shaft thin enough for my shoulders to touch the sides as I climb. Finally, I see the night sky and we exit into a vast expanse of concrete.

'It's a holding basin for the city's water,' Ash explains. 'Hasn't been used for years.'

We run up the sloping wall and crouch at the top to look over the edge.

A three-metre-high wire fence stretches as far as we can see, curving away into the darkness. A bitumen road runs between derelict houses, leading to two large gates, protected by a maze of bollards. In the front yard of one of the houses hooded figures huddle around an open fire. Strangest of all, there's something I haven't heard in years—music. Someone is playing a guitar and people are singing a song that sounds familiar.

JT and I smile at each other for the first time in two days. 'I miss music so much,' he says.

'Yeah, me too.'

I don't remember the name of the song, but it sets off a kaleidoscope of memories: images of Mum dancing around the kitchen, Dad using a wooden spoon as a microphone, both of them singing at the top of their lungs.

'Come on,' Sarisi says, nudging us into action. 'Let's get closer.'

JT is first to his feet. He leans down and offers me his hand. I take it and he pulls me up close to his face. 'You and me,' he says. 'Together.'

Willow nudges him. 'And me,' she says.

'Yeah,' JT says. 'And you.'

We drop below the lip of the basin and move in the direction of the gates. When we climb to the top again, we're nearer to the fence.

'Fence three,' Ash says. 'The last one before the city.'

'And those people?' I ask.

'Workers who haven't been certified yet. They're waiting for their IDs. Mostly survivors from out west. Once they get IDs they can enter the city, and move into one of the protected suburbs.'

'How do they get an ID?' I ask.

'Four clean health checks in a month and someone inside to vouch for them,' Ash says.

'But you called them workers,' JT says.

'Between here and the city, there are small farms. They're

allowed in each day to work but they've got to be out by curfew.'

'Is that how we get in?' I ask.

'Kinda,' Sarisi says.

The house is a shell, everything stripped out of it. The carpet stinks and the walls are covered with graffiti. We've been here most of the night, waiting for Sarisi to return. Finally, not long before dawn, she steps through the door with a hooded and masked figure.

'This them?' a muffled voice asks.

Sarisi nods.

'Five? It's a lot to get through unnoticed.' It's a boy's voice. He's tall, but his clothes hang off him. His wrists are thin where they poke out from his sleeves and he wears fingerless gloves. 'We'll need payment,' he says.

'They don't have anything,' Sarisi says.

'They have that,' he says, pointing at the rifle.

'No way.' JT is on his feet. 'We're not trading it.'

'Okay,' the boy replies, and he turns and walks out the door.

'Wait. Wait,' Ash calls, pulling him back.

Ash takes JT and me aside. 'It's the only way,' he says. 'We'll never find Daymu unless we get inside. Please.'

'We'll have nothing to defend ourselves with,' JT replies.

Sarisi joins the conversation. 'We can't get it through the gate without being seen. We'd have to leave it here anyway.'

We've carried the rifle a long way and it'd be invaluable if we ever made it back to Angowrie. But that seems so far away I can't even think about it.

'Okay,' I say.

JT is reluctant but he hands the rifle to Ash.

The guy in the hoodie takes it and checks the bolt. He's familiar with weapons. 'Ammo?' he asks. I empty my pockets and give him the bullets. 'Be ready in half an hour,' he says. 'Faces covered. And you two,'—he points at JT and me—'make sure your hands are in your pockets. If they spot those trackers...'

We haven't slept all night and every muscle aches. My clothes are still damp from walking in the creek and the stitches in my chin itch. Willow sees me touching them. 'It's a good sign,' she says. 'Means it's healing.'

Before long, there's movement outside. A crowd of about thirty people has gathered by the gates. The hooded boy, who Ash calls Rory, leads us into the middle of the group. It feels instantly strange—I haven't been around this many people in years.

'Some extra passengers this morning,' he says, and everybody turns to look at us. They are dressed in a wild assortment of clothes, and there's a collective stench to them, like vinegar and piss. All have their faces covered but there's a lot you can tell from people's eyes. There are hard stares and soft smiles that show in the lines at the sides. I try not to be obvious but I can't help checking their eyes for signs of yellowing.

'Spread them out,' Rory says and we are pulled apart and shuffled along as the group forms a line. Willow is half a dozen places ahead of me. She's hidden the arrows under her shirt and taken the string from her bow, which she holds like a walking stick.

Through the fence, I see a military vehicle approach, the sun emerging from the horizon behind it. Dust fills the air as it pulls up. A smaller gate to the side of the large ones is opened and the line begins to move. There's a soldier on each side. They wear surgical masks, and they raise their voices, counting. But just as Willow is about to step through the gate, they stop. One points at the bow.

'You there,' he says to Willow, who pretends not to hear him.

'Hey, captain,' Rory calls from behind us, his voice loud, demanding. 'When are we getting those water tanks you promised. We can't pass health checks drinking shitty water.'

'When we're good and ready,' the soldier replies, his voice muffled by his mask.

I push forward and force those ahead of me to shuffle through.

'Here,' Rory says, throwing him a plastic bottle full of murky water. 'You try drinking this.'

'Fuck off, Rory,' the other soldier joins in.

'Easy for you to say, soldier boy.' Rory is getting more animated, throwing his arms around, forcing them to look at him. 'I bet you go home to clean water and a hot meal. Probably some nice Siley girl in your bed, too.'

This brings laughter and jeers.

'Shut up, Rory. I'm trying to count.'

'What, did you run out of fingers?' Rory scoffs.

Willow has kept walking and is now ten metres clear of the guards. The group closes around her and her bow disappears from view. The rest of us make it through unnoticed and are swallowed in the crowd.

I hear the gate creak behind us and a lock snapped into place.

'Get moving,' the captain calls. 'And, oh,' he says, putting on an American accent, 'have a nice day.'

We move off the road to allow the vehicle through. The driver fishtails, shooting stones and dust into our faces. Once it's out of sight, Sarisi pulls us from the group and we stop on the side of the road. The others continue without bothering to look back. Only Rory stops.

'Thanks,' I say. 'You saved us.'

'Worth the rifle, then?' he says.

'Yeah, worth the rifle.'

He removes the glove from his left hand and turns it to show the scar across the back, before jogging to catch the others.

'Where are the farms?' I ask Ash.

'Closer to the city,' he says. 'About an hour's walk.'

'Is that where we're heading?'

'No, we're going to the river. There are patrols so we'll have to stay off the roads. Getting through the gate was the easy bit,' he says.

Sarisi leads us away from the road. 'We need to stick close to the fence,' she says. 'Keep an ear out for drones.'

The sun has only been up for half an hour but the morning is already hot. We move at a fast pace. The sweat pours off me. Willow has restrung her bow—it's our only weapon now.

From the top of a stony ridge, we get our first view of the outskirts of Wentworth. It's totally different from what I remember travelling in on the school bus each morning. Back then, the farms ran right up to the new housing subdivisions that were gradually pushing south towards the coast. The hills were covered with trees and there were parks and shopping centres and football ovals. Now, whole areas look abandoned, the skeletons of houses stripped of any useful materials, their frames and roof beams exposed.

'It's not all like this,' Sarisi says. 'Everyone lives closer in. Safety in numbers.'

We reach the first of the protected suburbs by mid-morning. A paling fence follows the lie of the land, separating the houses from the dry country beyond. We edge closer, hiding behind rocks and fallen trees as we go. From here I pick up the sound of something so familiar I can almost picture the scene before we climb the fence and get a view of the road. Two kids, a boy and a girl, stand a few metres apart, talking and kicking a football between them. There's the sound of shoes on leather and the slap of the ball hitting hands. Every now and then the boy tucks the ball under his arm, raising his voice to make a point. The girl shrugs and the kick-to-kick continues. They're dressed in shorts and T-shirts. Their runners are dirty, but their hair is neat, the girl's in a ponytail and the boy's swept back off his face. They play in front of a house, one of half a dozen on the street that look inhabited. The windows are all intact, there's some grass and a garden, and the front door is open. I pick up the smell of food cooking.

'Harley,' a man's voice calls from inside. 'Come and eat, son.'

Those words are enough to make my heart flip—kids playing,

food cooking, a dad calling. This is what I remember, what I long for.

'Can Maddy stay for lunch?' the boy asks.

A man appears in the doorway, a tea towel over his shoulder. 'Sure, she can,' he says, smiling at the girl. 'Just let your mum know, Maddy.'

JT is next to me. We climb back down and lean against the fence. I suddenly ache for Mum and Dad, for all the little minutes that made up our lives—the conversations, the meals, the jokes and the arguments. I think I'd give anything to be that boy, to walk into that house, sit at a table and share a meal. Is this what life in Wentworth is like now?

Willow interrupts my thoughts. 'How much further?' she asks Sarisi.

'We're here,' she says, jabbing a stick into the dirt. 'And this is the river.' She draws a squiggly line a metre to the left. 'And here'—she moves the stick beyond the river—'is where the factories and the convent are. There's no guarantee Kas and Daymu will be there—they could have been on-sold by now—but if they only arrived recently, chances are they'll be on work details.'

'Doing what?' I ask.

'Working in the laundries or the abattoirs,' she says.

'All the shit jobs no one else wants to do, you mean?'

'Yeah. So *they* can live like *that*,' she says, pointing past the fence to the houses.

17

We skirt around the back of the houses towards the river.

'We can get close this afternoon but we'll have to wait for dark before we cross,' Sarisi says.

'What happens when we don't pass back through the check-point tonight?' I ask.

'We've got that covered. There are a dozen or so workers roaming loose inside the fence. The army doesn't keep track of who's who. They go on the numbers in and out.'

'Smart,' JT says.

'There's an underground network operating right under their noses,' she says. 'They reckon they're in control if no one's openly fighting back.'

'What about the No-landers?' Willow says.

'The No-landers are dangerous,' Ash replies. 'They think the only way to fight is openly. They give the army a reason to put up with Ramage and his mob.'

Ash is right. There's more than one way to fight.

We walk for another hour until we reach the edge of what must once have been a series of sports ovals on the south side of the river. They've all been dug over and rows of vegetables push up through the dark soil. There are tomatoes, potatoes, melons and capsicums. Closer to the water, pumpkins spread along the fallen branches of redgums, and broad beans stand like rows of green soldiers. My mind throws back to Dad planting them in the backyard. He always said if you couldn't grow broad beans you should forget about gardening altogether.

'We'll wait out the afternoon here,' Sarisi says, directing us into the shade of a cypress hedge that's lost its shape. Branches fork out at odd angles and dry needles blanket the ground. Ash passes around a water bottle. There's a thick layer of sediment in the bottom but we're so thirsty we hardly care.

I look back the way we've come. All day I've had the feeling we're being followed—something in the way the shadows move, like there's someone watching, just out of sight. It makes me nervous.

'What are you looking for?' Ash asks.

'Dunno. I keep thinking someone's following us.'

'You're paranoid,' he says, peering into the dust swirling in the wind. 'There's nothing out there.'

Willow sits with JT and me. Her face above her mask is black with dirt and her hair stands out like a scarecrow's. She runs a finger along her bowstring and rests a hand on the bunched arrows by her side.

Each of us finds a spot to lie under the hedge. Willow crawls in next to me. I can't remember when I last slept and even though I'm shit-scared now that we're inside the fence, I drop into an exhausted sleep.

Again, I dream of Kas. I'm trying to run towards her across a stony field, but my bare feet are bloody and bruised. Just as I get close enough to touch her, Tusker appears and pulls her out of reach, his hands all over her, his mouth at her neck, kissing her. I wake with a start, hot and sweating.

It takes me a few seconds to get my bearings again, but the image of Kas being dragged away stays with me.

I've slept longer than I thought—it's late afternoon. Without thinking, I walk to the other side of the hedge to take a piss. Above the wind, I hear a whirring sound, and a drone appears, heading straight for me. I dive for cover but it comes in low and hovers directly above me. Something fizzes past my shoulder, followed by the sound of metal hitting metal.

Willow has shot the drone with an arrow!

It spins in circles tilting wildly as it tries to right itself, but Willow has reloaded, and she's hit it again. This arrow catches one of the propellers and the drone crashes to the ground. Sarisi hits it with a tree branch, breaking it into half a dozen pieces.

We stand above the mangled wreck. A tiny green light on the underbelly flashes then dies. We look at each other, trying to figure out the consequences of what we've done.

'Would they have seen us?' I ask.

'Probably,' Ash says. 'I don't know whether they record data or they transmit live. It looks pretty old-school, like it's been patched together.'

'Whatever,' Sarisi says, 'we'll have to take a chance on getting down to the river in daylight.'

Willow has been standing off to the side. 'I'm sorry,' she says.

Sarisi smiles. 'It'd already spotted Finn. You did the right thing.'

Willow stands a little taller. She retrieves the two arrows. One is snapped in half but the other one is fine.

There's more urgency as Sarisi leads us through the paddock towards the river. We get some cover from the trellises strung with tomato plants, but they've already been stripped of their fruit and the leaves are starting to die off. Once we make it to the broad beans, we're completely hidden. JT nudges me and points to the thick pods hanging off the plants around us. We start picking, grabbing handfuls, splitting the casings to find the fat, green beans inside. We haven't eaten all day and we push handfuls into our mouths. The outer skin is bitter but the centre is sweet. We move along the rows on our hands and knees, picking madly and filling our pockets.

Ash goes ahead to check the best way to the water. The sun is beginning to drop in the west. It struggles to penetrate the dust lifting off the plains and everything around us is lit in an amber glow.

Ash returns with a worried look on his face.

'What is it?' Sarisi asks.

Ash signals us to move to the end of the row. He points. Five soldiers are clearly visible on the hill, standing above the remains of the drone. They disappear behind the hedge for a minute, then reappear, moving in slow, deliberate circles, checking the ground for tracks.

Sarisi leads us quickly back into the beans where we push through row after row, until the ground begins to drop towards the river. There's a ten-metre gap between the last row and the red gums lining the bank. We sprint across and throw ourselves down the slope into the reeds. Our ankles sink in the mud, but we push out further until we're wading in the shallows. The water is cool against our parched skin and I wet my hair and bunch it in my hands to pull it away from my face. Willow sinks chest-deep, and JT reaches a hand to her. She grabs hold and the two of them edge along parallel to the bank.

We can hear voices now. The soldiers have tracked us to the vegetable plots. Sarisi is beside us. She puts her fingers to her lips and passes us lengths of hollow reed she's broken off. She puts one in her mouth, holds her nose and sinks below the surface.

Willow looks at me, her eyes flashing left and right, and I nod to reassure her. *We can do this*, I mouth. I loop my arm through hers, put the reed between my teeth and lower myself under the water.

I start by holding my breath but eventually I test the reed. It works. Willow is fretting next to me, pulling at my arm. I resurface and find her gasping for air. The voices are closer now and heavy boots crash along the bank. Willow is panicking, her breath coming in ragged bursts. I take her by the shoulders and force her to look at me. I put the reed back in her mouth and get her to breathe through it before we go under again. She's still holding me but her grip is more relaxed.

I don't know how long we stay like this. I resurface every couple of minutes to listen for the soldiers. The coolness of the river has become a deep cold that's worked its way into my bones. The next time I come up, the others have surfaced too. We wait and listen for a few more minutes, but all we can hear are the movement of leaves in the breeze and the distant ringing of a bell.

'Curfew,' Sarisi says. 'The lights will be on soon.'

We wade parallel to the bank for about fifty metres before struggling through the reeds like rats looking for dry land. We crawl into the space beneath the low branch of a red gum.

Willow is shivering and I can't stop my teeth chattering. We hug each other for the body warmth.

'What now?' I stutter, struggling to control my breath.

'We have to cross the river,' Sarisi says. Her clothes stick to her, and I can see the bunched muscles of her arms.

'What about the soldiers?' I ask. I wish I could stop my body from shaking.

'There are always people trying to raid the vegetable plots for extra food,' she says. 'The soldiers will probably stay and guard them.'

'Do we swim across the river?' JT says. He's trying to control his voice too, but there's a waver in it.

'No,' Ash replies. 'We're too cold, now. The bridges are all guarded, but we know a way. Let's go.'

We stay below the high bank, climbing over debris and fallen branches. Eventually we pass under the first bridge and come out onto a path that seems safe to use now that night has fallen.

'It's an old bike track,' Ash says.

Ahead of us, another bridge appears. When we get closer, I see it's actually a huge pipe stretching across the river.

'There's a metal gantry along one side,' Sarisi says. 'It's rusted out in places, so you have to watch your step, but it's usually unguarded.'

'Usually?' I say.

'Yeah, no guarantees.'

To access the crossing, we have to climb the bank. Sarisi tells us to wait. We sit and watch, wondering why we're not crossing straightaway.

Then, as we look over the river towards the main part of town, the lights blink, blink again, and then hold. Everything on our side is left dark.

'They've shut down most of the circuits to save power,' Sarisi says. 'They only light what they have to. All the factories start up for two hours.'

'Why don't they use power during the day?' I ask.

'They can work outside then—farming mostly, and rein-forcing the fences.'

There's something beautiful about the patterns of light. They seem so strange after the years of darkness. But here they are, lighting streets and corners, houses and factories. The town looks like its own little galaxy. Even with all the chaos and fear rippling around us, it glows with hope and a sense of purpose. It's mesmerising.

I turn and peer into the darkness behind us. The feeling of being watched hasn't left me.

'Come on,' Sarisi says. 'Time to move.'

The gantry is only a metre wide and every so often it disappears altogether where it's rusted and fallen into the river. I try not to think of how far the drop might be. Willow is in front of me, her bow bobbing above her head. The gaps are mostly narrow enough to jump but a couple of them are too wide and we're forced up onto the pipe, which is curved and slippery. We're much more exposed up here.

Nearing the other side, Sarisi disappears towards the lights to check things out. We catch our breath and huddle next to the pipe until she whistles us across.

Stepping off the bridge is like entering a different world. The streetlights cast a hazy orange glow over the trees and buildings. This side of the river is lined with the red-brick walls of factories. We can hear the hum of machinery. We keep to the shadows for as long as we can, staying close to the water, until Sarisi turns into an unlit laneway between buildings. It opens onto a wide street, where the wrecks of cars have been pushed to the side to allow vehicles a clearway. A truck swings around the corner ahead of us, its headlights bouncing off broken glass and strips of metal pulled loose from the cars. We flatten ourselves against the wall, and the truck passes through the high gates of a factory further along the street.

'Sileys,' Sarisi says. JT and I exchange glances. 'They bring them here every night while the power's on. They'll work until the lights go out. This is a slaughterhouse,' she says, matter-of-factly.

'So,' I say, hardly daring to hope, 'Kas and Daymu could be with them?'

'Maybe. This is where the new arrivals usually work.'

'They would've only been here a couple of weeks,' JT says. I can hear the hope in his voice.

We cross the footpath to gain cover behind the car wrecks and run low and hard until we're opposite the open gates. The truck is nowhere to be seen, but we can still hear the motor running.

'You sure you want to do this?' Sarisi asks. 'If you're caught here, there'll be no escaping.'

JT and I nod. Ash is silent but the look on his face gives Sarisi her answer. Willow is focused on the gates. She doesn't look nervous, but she's breathing heavily.

'How do we do this?' I ask Sarisi.

'We can get inside though the loading dock. There's a corridor that passes the killing floor and leads to the boning room. If they're here, that's where they'll most likely be.'

'Sounds like you've been here before,' JT says.

She looks away. 'We can climb to a platform above the boning room,' she says. 'No use risking our skins if they're not there.'

The street is deserted. One at a time, we run to the factory wall and slip inside the gates. As we get closer to the building, the stench of blood and shit fills our nostrils. We pull the rags over our mouths and noses and climb into the loading bay. It's like entering hell, hot and reeking of death. We can hear the frantic squealing of animals.

'Pigs,' Sarisi says.

Inside, the air is even thicker. On one side there are narrow chutes for the animals but Sarisi signals us through the curtain of plastic strips hanging from the ceiling. Behind it, a series of passages, dark and sticky with blood, leads us further into the building. I slip and fall, feeling the thick liquid seep into my clothes. Even with my face covered, I gag every few seconds, the taste of broad beans filling my mouth. The squealing gets louder, echoing through the building.

At the end of a long, sloping passageway, Sarisi climbs a ladder and we follow. At the top, a rough wooden platform extends out over a brightly lit room.

There are soldiers with rifles at each end and about twenty people are spread out along a wide, stainless-steel bench. They watch a man wearing a heavy leather apron cut the meat from a pig carcass that hangs from a sliding rail above him. He grips the shoulder of the animal and slips the knife in, half pulling, half sawing the flesh until a bloodied lump drops onto the table. He slides the cut piece of meat along the line and the others go to work on it with long boning knives.

All the workers look alike: their hair is pulled up under plastic caps, masks cover their faces and their dark blue coveralls are splattered with blood and gristle. My eyes move over them, one at a time. They're only ten metres away but half of them have their backs to us. I look at their body shape and height, trying to match them to Kas or Daymu.

Willow grabs my arm. She points to a gap in the boards. I put my cheek against the rough timber and peer through. Two figures are getting ready, pulling on their caps. Their masks are on a chair next to them. As one tilts her head back to bunch her hair in her hands, her birthmark catches the light. It's Kas, and Daymu is next to her, climbing into too-big coveralls.

My heart leaps. They're here! We've found them.

Then I notice a third figure standing on a step above them, arms crossed tight against her chest.

It's Bridget Monahan.

18

Kas is so close I could reach out and touch her. I roll onto my side and stare at JT. He's seen them too. We point to show Sarisi, and she nods before pulling us towards the ladder. I don't want to leave Kas, but we have to work out what to do next. We retrace our steps to the loading bay, the stench rolling over us in hot waves. Dropping into the yard we creep around the corner to where the truck is parked by the side entrance. There's no sign of the driver.

'This is where they'll come out,' Sarisi says. 'The factory lights will be off by then. There'll be a couple of torches but mostly they'll rely on the truck headlights. They're blinding when you walk towards them. It's our best chance to get to Kas and Daymu.'

'But how?' JT asks. 'Those soldiers were armed.'

'We'll take out the headlights. The rest is up to you,' Sarisi says.

She leads us through a maze of rotting wooden pallets to a spot where the factory wall has collapsed. Bricks are scattered on the ground. 'We'll use these,' she says.

'Bricks against bullets,' I say. 'I don't like our chances.'

'Have you got a better idea?' she asks.

I don't. I'm not thinking clearly after seeing Kas. I lean against the wall and drag clean air into my lungs.

Sarisi outlines her plan. JT, Willow and I will hide inside the entrance. We'll signal when Kas and Daymu approach and grab them when Sarisi and Ash take out the headlights with the bricks. Then we run.

We all know it's a shit plan. The only thing we have going for us is the element of surprise. Otherwise, we're outgunned and outnumbered. They could raise the alarm and within ten minutes have half the army chasing us through a town we're not familiar with.

We agree to meet back at the pipe over the river.

Ash pulls JT aside and puts a hand on his shoulder. 'Get her,' he implores. 'Get Daymu.'

JT, Willow and I pull rags over our faces again and slip through the entrance, making our way along a wide corridor that ends in a staircase. They will have to come down it from the boning room. We hide along the side, crouching in the dark, and wait. The small space concentrates the stench that seems to inhabit every corner of the building. It hangs in the air and makes us gag.

Time drags. It must be close to lights out. My stomach aches for food and my legs cramp from squatting against the wall. My throat is dry and I'd give anything for even a mouthful of water.

Willow sits next to me. She punches her thighs to stop her legs shaking. She looks up at me and my heart burns with the sight of her. Her lips are tight and she scrapes the hair back behind her ears. She rests the bow across her knees and fits an arrow into place.

After what seems an eternity, the hum of machinery slows and grinds to a halt. The whole building seems to shudder with an exhausted sigh. We jump to our feet. Adrenaline courses through me. Boots thump down the wooden stairs, and two soldiers walk out through the doors to the truck. The engine rumbles to life and the building plunges into momentary darkness before the corridor is flooded with the headlights from the truck.

More footsteps on the stairs above us, moving past in twos and threes. From the shadows, we search their faces for Kas and Daymu. They're at the back of the group, which is now spread out along the corridor.

Suddenly, there's the sound of breaking glass and everything is black again. Ash and Sarisi have taken out the headlights. There's shouting and confusion as bodies collide. We elbow our way into the crowd. JT grabs Daymu, and I put my arm around Kas. She swings wildly with her fist and connects below my ribs. I'm half-winded but I pull her into a headlock and whisper, 'Kas! It's me.'

Her body jerks with the sound of my voice and I pull her back below the stairs where Willow waits. Daymu and JT land on top of us.

There's more shouting and screaming in the corridor now, and sweeping beams of torchlight. The Sileys barge towards the door, knocking aside anyone in their way. Outside, rifle fire rips the air. We cringe back into the dark, our bodies hot and sweaty and stinking of meat.

The corridor empties out. I can imagine the Sileys running blind, trying to find the gates, tripping over each other at the chance at freedom.

Kas finds my face in the dark. She squeezes her hands against my cheeks, her mouth close to mine. 'I knew you'd come,' she says. 'I *knew* you would.'

I can't find the words to tell her how much I've missed her, how much I've ached for her. I put my arms around her and kiss her again and again. I can't tell whether Daymu is laughing or crying, but she has pinned JT to the wall and he holds her face to his chest.

Willow finds us and pushes into Kas.

'Wils,' Kas whispers. 'What are you doing here?'

'Someone had to organise this rescue,' Willow says, only half-joking.

My chest could burst with the excitement and fear and something that might be love.

We regroup in the corridor trying to figure the best way out.

We're about to move towards the door when a beam of light pierces the dark from the top of the stairs. The light bounces off the wall and I make out the heavy features of Bridget Monahan.

'Can't say I'm surprised,' she says, the treads creaking under her weight as she descends. 'Thought you might come looking for *my* girls.'

I've got my hand across my face, shielding my eyes from the glare.

Bridget tilts her head to the side. 'You're brave, I'll give you that—coming into Wentworth.' She shines the light on Willow and sees she has her bow drawn back and an arrow ready to shoot. 'It's okay, luv,' she says. 'You won't need that.'

There are voices outside the door and torches shine onto the ceiling. 'Get back in there,' Bridget says, pointing under the stairs. 'Trust me.'

'We trusted you once before, remember,' Kas says.

'That was different. That was Ramage.'

We hesitate.

'Quick,' she whispers. 'They're coming.'

I doubt we can trust her but we've got no other option. We crowd into the recess as Bridget walks towards the door. It opens before she gets there and more torchlight streams into the corridor.

'All clear here,' she yells, her voice filled with authority. The soldiers back away and we're left in the quiet.

When we climb out, Kas takes my hand. Hers is sticky with blood. She presses her face against mine. Her cheeks are wet.

'Finn,' she says, relief in her voice. 'Ahh, Finn.'

'How do we get out of here?' JT's voice snaps us back to the danger that's all around us.

'We've only used this one entrance,' Kas says. 'I don't know any other way out.'

'Can you get us back to the boning room from here?' I ask her.

'I can,' Daymu says. 'Follow me.'

We sprint up the stairs and Daymu takes us through a network of corridors as our eyes adjust to the dark. In the boning room rats lick blood off the floor, hardly bothering to move as we pass under the platform to the base of the ladder. From there, we retrace our steps to the loading bay.

The yard is empty. All the action seems to have moved out into the surrounding streets. There's the sound of gunshots and shouting. I take the lead now, through the gates, across the road, down the alleyway and onto the river path. Kas is beside me all the way and she runs holding hands with Willow.

The moon has risen and casts enough light for us to see the pipe across the river. We approach cautiously. Two figures appear out of the trees and step onto the path. Sarisi smiles. 'Not such a bad plan after all, huh?' she says.

Ash pushes past her and stops in front of Daymu. The moonlight shines on his face and Daymu launches herself at him. He picks her up, hugging her and pushing his face into her hair.

'You have to go,' Sarisi says. 'This side of the river is crawling with patrols.'

'You're not coming?' I say.

She stays silent for a few seconds. 'There are others who need my help,' she says. 'Ash can get you back to the fence.'

'Thank you,' I say, putting my hand out for her to shake. She nods, touches the tips of my fingers with hers and moves down the line. The others whisper their thanks.

When she reaches Ash, she says, 'What will you do?'

'I'm going with Daymu,' he says.

They embrace, and then Sarisi melts into the dark.

The bridge is more exposed with the moon up—the gantry is clearly lit.

We climb the bank and wait for everyone to gather at the top. There are six of us now. That's six chances of being spotted.

'I think we should cross two at a time,' I say. 'They could be waiting on the other side. I'll go first with Kas, then Willow and JT, then Ash and Daymu. Watch for the gaps. I'll whistle if it's safe to cross.'

I don't know where this plan comes from, but I hope it sounds reasonable. No one argues, so I step onto the gantry with Kas close behind. We run forty metres to the first gap, climb up onto the pipe to get around it and drop back to the gantry.

For the first time I'm daring to think we might get away with this. The army will be occupied with chasing the escaped Sileys. If we can make it to the other side of the river and retrace our steps to the fence, who knows what's possible? But as we land on the gantry, I make out a shape ahead of us. I barely have time to warn Kas before it stands and takes form in front of me. It's a man, and the rifle he holds is pointed at my chest.

'Bet you thought you'd seen the last of me,' Tusker says.

I'm frozen to the spot, gripping the rail on the side of the pipe with one hand and reaching for Kas with the other.

Tusker steps out of the shadows and into light. He's beaming, with all his teeth showing, and chuckling to himself. 'Oh, you thought you were so clever,' he says, hardly able to contain himself. 'I've been following you all day. Watched you sneaking across the river like rats, so I knew you'd be back this way eventually.' He's close enough for me to pick out every feature, the thick scar running down the side of his face, the grizzled beard and the curl of his lip. 'And I'm guessing the others are over there,' he says, nudging the rifle towards the bank behind us.

I'm blocking his view of Kas but he knows she's there. 'And you've brought my girlfriend as well,' he says wetting his lips with his tongue. 'Ooh, Kas.' He draws out the s sound like a snake. 'Have I got plans for you.' He nudges me with the barrel of the rifle to move me aside. 'I knew he'd lead me to you,' he says to her.

My hunch was right all along. We were being followed.

'You know what they call me?' he asks. 'The other Wilders?'

I can only shake my head. I don't feel afraid, just angry. I've come this far, found Kas, beaten the odds. And now here he is again, standing in our way, trying to make me feel small and worthless.

'The panther,' he says. 'That's what they call me. The killer no one sees coming.'

The anger rises and spills out my mouth. 'Panther! You're kidding. You're a bag of shit, Tusker.'

He tilts his head. 'Then how come you didn't see me?' he sneers.

Behind me I hear the creak of iron as Kas lets go of my hand and starts to back away, looking to escape. But Tusker sees her. He brings the rifle to my forehead and tells me to kneel, exposing Kas. 'One more step, girl,' he says, 'and his brains will be in the river.'

Kas says nothing, but I feel her move closer.

'Here's what we're going to do,' he says, his voice calmer now. He takes a step backwards. 'You, boy, are going for a swim. Stand up!'

I'm looking for any opportunity to lunge for the rifle, but he's put too much distance between us. My knees are shaking and I need to pull on the rail to get to my feet. 'Good boy,' he says. 'Now, don't spoil everything by trying something stupid.'

'You're not supposed to be here, are you?' Kas says loudly. She's trying to stall him.

'The army's losing control. It's every man for himself,' he says.

'Losing control?' Kas says, and I can imagine the smirk on her face. 'You mean they've finally worked out what you and Ramage have been up to. You're on the run, aren't you?'

'Enough talk,' he shouts. 'You're coming with me. We've got unfinished business. I can't wait to see you—'

'And Finn?' Kas interrupts.

'Him?' Tusker says. He spits at me. 'He's excess baggage.'

He leans forward, the rifle still pointed at Kas, and grabs a handful of my hair. He's so strong I feel like a ragdoll in his grip. He pulls me to a break in the rail and wrenches me sideways until I'm on the edge looking into the darkness below.

There's a moment when everything seems to slow. Faces flash through my head—Rose sitting at the table in Angowrie, Ray by the fire at his place, scratching Rowdy under the chin, Harry and Stella standing by the gate at the valley farm, cradling Hope in their arms. And Kas, wet and naked on the beach—everyone I love and care for, everyone I want to protect.

There's no thought to what I do, no plan—it's an explosion of rage. My foot finds a ridge in the metal gantry and I lever myself off it, taking hold of Tusker's belt, tilting him towards the edge. The butt of the rifle clips my shoulder, but he's taken the weight off one foot. I pull with all my strength. And then we're in midair, freefalling towards the water.

19

The fall seems to take forever. If I was jumping in daylight, I'd know when to brace for the impact but we're tumbling in the dark.

I'm on top of Tusker when we finally hit with a dull *oomph* sound as the air is knocked out of me. Something wrenches in my shoulder but the shock of the cold water instantly dulls the pain. I have time to take one quick breath before Tusker drags me down. He thrashes his arms and legs, the weight of his clothes pulling him under. The rifle is gone. I've still got hold of his belt and he claws at me in his efforts to find the surface. I don't know how far under we are, but I stay clearheaded enough to let the air out of my lungs slowly, preserving oxygen. Letting go of his belt, I kick him as hard as I can to get clear. When I've created some space between us I go where I know he won't follow—deeper.

Something hard touches my back—one of the bridge supports. There's a ledge where I can pin my foot to hold my position. Tusker is a vague shape now, his arms reaching up like he's climbing a ladder, but still he sinks. I can just make him out, his hair fanning wildly around his face and bubbles streaming from his nose. I wedge my foot harder under the ledge and watch him struggle.

Eventually, he stops thrashing, his eyes wide with terror and his open mouth taking in water. His body is still upright, like he knows where the surface is, but there's no fight left in him. He floats away in the slow current, disappearing like a ghost into the murk.

I close my eyes but still he's there, his lifeless stare accusing me, judging me for not saving him.

I'm running out of oxygen and my mind drifts. I'm in the rock pool with Kas, sitting on the bottom, smiling at her as she tries to outlast me. My lungs are almost empty and now I see the sun filtering down into the pool. Kas's legs move in a slow kicking motion towards the surface. I release my foot from the ledge and push up towards her, swimming hard.

I'm barely aware of breaking the surface. I lie on my back and gulp at the air. The stars are out and I focus on the shimmering dots studding the sky. I could stay here forever, I think, just me and the water and the stars and the oxygen spreading through my body.

It's as though my ears have been blocked but gradually I become aware of voices somewhere above me. On the bridge?

'Finn,' someone calls and it sounds like they're afraid to shout. But I'd know that voice anywhere.

'What?' I say, not even sure if it's loud enough for Kas to hear.

There are little yips of joy and excited voices above. 'Can you swim to the far bank?' she asks.

'Yeah,' I say but as I go to swing my shoulder over, a stabbing pain rips through it, radiating down my arm. I touch it with my hand and feel the bulge at the side of the socket where it's dislocated. As though my body's only now become aware of it, the pain swells and pulses. I grit my teeth and, with my injured shoulder on top, sidestroke towards the bank. It takes me ages and by the time I'm close, three figures have waded out to meet me.

'Are you all right?' JT asks, reaching for me. I scream as he pulls on my arm. 'Shit! Sorry,' he says.

Finally, I feel the mud under my feet and I stagger onto the bank. Kas has her arm looped around my waist and she helps me sit down.

'Tusker?' she asks.

I can't find the words yet to tell her what happened. I can hardly believe it myself—or even begin to understand that he's gone.

'Where are you hurt?' Willow asks.

I carefully pull the T-shirt off my shoulder. The bone bulges awkwardly to the side of the socket.

'Dislocated!' JT says. He sounds almost excited. 'Used to happen to me all the time playing football. Sometimes it'd just pop out while I was running.'

'Spare me the detail,' I say. 'Can you put it back in?'

'No problem, but it's gonna hurt like shit.'

'It hurts worse than shit, now.'

He carefully takes my arm in both hands, bends my elbow up and pulls away from the shoulder. Then he rotates my forearm. I clench my teeth hard to stop from screaming. With a final twist and pull that shoots pain across my back and up into my neck, I feel it slide back into place. It still aches, but the pain is different—bearable.

JT makes a sling out of my T-shirt.

Kas sits beside me, her arm still locked around my waist.

Daymu is higher on the bank, looking around. 'Where to now?' she calls.

Ash says, 'We have to get back to the fence. I don't know how we'll get through, but...'

'How far is it?' Kas asks.

'If we walk through the night we could make it before sunrise. We'd have to take a direct route. It's quicker but more dangerous.'

'Sooner we get going, the better,' JT says.

We leave the river and jog across a huge expanse of bitumen car park. Every footfall sends a bolt of pain through my shoulder and I have to run doubled over to protect it. The signage has fallen off the building on the other side of the car park but the outline remains:

WENTWORTH WEST COMMUNITY CENTRE.

For the first time in days, I know where we are. The town is so different now I've been disorientated, but I remember this place. There used to be a market here on Sundays. I came with Mum sometimes when she volunteered on a stall for some environmental group.

We're halfway across when the whole area is suddenly lit. Half a dozen vehicles surround us, trapping us in their glare.

'On the ground! Now!' The order comes from somewhere to our right. We drop to our knees. Heavy boots come towards us out of the light, and strong hands pull us apart. I cry out when my shoulder is knocked.

'All right, take it easy,' one of the voices says.

'Are you sure it's him?' a deeper voice asks.

'Yeah, it's him.'

The motor of one of the trucks turns over and it rolls towards us. I expect us to be separated but we're all loaded into the back. We sit along the sides in the muted light, looking into each other's faces. Ash slumps with his head in his hands, Daymu's arm around his shoulder. 'We were so close,' he says. 'So close.'

Two armed guards climb in behind and the truck begins to move. I feel like all the air has been pushed out of me. Muscles that have been as tight as wire let go and I hug my good arm to my chest. Kas sits opposite. She leans forward and puts her hands on my knees. She looks different—her hair is shorter, her clothes are a better fit and she's wearing a new pair of runners. Her birthmark is lighter, or maybe her skin is darker, I can't tell. I want to ask her what's happened since we were captured at Devils Elbow, but for now all I have the energy to do is lean into her until our foreheads touch. She strokes my cheek with the back of her hand and I feel like I could die with the touch of it. She runs a finger along my chapped lips then kisses me softly.

The truck crosses the river and the driver grinds through the gears as we climb a hill, before swinging away to the right.

'This isn't the way to the convent,' Kas whispers.

Willow sits with her knees pulled up to her chest. She wraps her arms around her legs. I realise it's the first time I've seen her without her bow in ages. She catches me looking and nods. 'They took it,' she says.

After about ten minutes we pass through heavy steel gates that close behind us. The truck pulls up in the middle of a courtyard inside high bluestone walls. The tailgate drops and we are herded out at gunpoint. I know this place. It's the old Wentworth jail. It was a tourist spot before the virus. We came here on an excursion in primary school once.

The six of us huddle together. The jail is dark but torchlights approach through a metal door to the side of the yard and three soldiers walk towards us.

'Which one of you is Finn Morrison?' one asks.

I'm so surprised to hear my name I don't answer for a few seconds. 'I am,' I say finally.

'Come with us.' I feel a rifle at my back and I'm led towards the door. The others are told to wait where they are, under guard.

'What's going on?' I ask but no one says anything.

A figure appears and blocks our way. He nods and smiles.

'G'day,' he says.

It's Winston, the soldier we last saw at the No-landers camp. 'I wanted to say thank you,' he says.

'No worries,' I say, even more confused. 'What's going on?' I ask again.

'Just follow me,' he says.

We walk along a narrow passage between two high walls, and then into another, smaller courtyard. On the other side we enter a room lit by kero lamps. A man sits behind a solid timber desk. His uniform is clean and the stripes at the shoulders show his rank. Winston points me to a chair, salutes and leaves the room.

The man pours a glass of water and passes it to me. I take it, spilling some as I gulp it down. My clothes are still wet from the river and my body shakes. He rises from his chair, picks up a blanket from a couch under the window and drapes it around my shoulders.

Sitting down again he has one elbow on the desk and his chin cupped in his hand. He looks about sixty, maybe a little younger, clean-shaven and with neatly combed hair greying at the sides. He looks like anyone's kindly grandfather. 'I'm General Dowling,' he says.

I've got no idea what to make of this so I stay quiet.

'We've been looking for you, Finn' he says. His voice is even and controlled. 'You've been hard to keep up with.'

'How do you know my name?' I say.

He tilts his head to the side. I've almost forgotten how my voice sounds to new people.

'You were arrested on the coast road near Megs Creek three weeks ago,' he says. 'You were taken to Longley, tried, sentenced and transported to Wentworth. Though, of course, you escaped, with the help of the rebels, so you never actually arrived here. Well, your tracker did, but it didn't seem to be attached to your hand anymore.'

I lift my left hand and turn the back to him. 'This tracker?' I say.

His face gives nothing away, but I've irritated him. 'You think you're pretty clever, don't you, Finn?'

'I'm just trying to survive. Like everyone else.'

'Everyone else doesn't harbour Sileys. They don't evade the decontamination squads. They don't torch army vehicles. They don't enter the city without authorisation. And they don't incite mass escapes. I'd say you've done quite a bit more than just survive.'

'If you're looking for an apology, you're not going to get one.'

He sits back in his chair and crosses his arms. 'Winston told me what happened at the rebel camp,' he says. 'It's the only reason we're having this conversation.'

'Then he must have told you it wasn't only me. JT and Willow helped him, too.'

He thinks on this for a while. 'What happened on the bridge tonight?' he asks. I get the sense he's circling me like a boxer looking for a weakness.

I try to form the words but nothing comes out. The image of Tusker's lifeless body floating off into darkness is too fresh in my mind. All I can do is shake my head.

'We've been looking for a man named Peter Tusker. Do you know him?'

'You know I do. He was at our trial in Longley.'

'Yes, but you knew him before then,' he says.

I've been ducking and weaving, but now I come out swinging. 'Tusker is a Wilder. He works for Ramage. They're slave traders, rapists and murderers, the worst of the worst.' I pull my sleeve up to show him the branding on my arm. 'This is how they treat kids.'

He tries to keep his face neutral, but his eyes widen when he sees the brand. He takes a deep breath and returns to his questioning. 'Did you see Tusker tonight?' he asks.

'Yes, on the bridge. He fell. He drowned.'

He nods, as though I'm only confirming what he already knows. He stands, walks around the desk and puts his hand on my good shoulder. I try to shrug it off. 'Finn, we can help each other.'

'Sorry?' I'm confused.

'Benjamin Ramage has been arrested and charged with corruption and perverting the course of justice.'

'What?' I say, hardly believing what I'm hearing.

'We've been watching him for months, and we have solid evidence against him. But we need more. Is there anything you can tell us about his operations immediately after the virus?'

I'm on my guard, again. My shoulder aches but I sit up straight and fix my eyes on a spot on the wall behind his head. This has to be a trap. I need to be careful.

'It's okay. I understand,' he says. 'Why should you trust

me? Every kind of authority has let you down for three years. I know you survived on your own in Angowrie. I know about the valley and I know about Hope.'

'But how?'

'That's not important at the moment.' He takes a deep breath and seems to hold it in his chest for a long time. The braids on his uniform quiver. 'Let me be perfectly clear here—your fate is in my hands, Finn.'

'If you've caught Ramage, does that mean we're free to go. Since it was him that convicted us.'

'No.' He answers quickly, like he's been expecting the question. 'Three of your companions are Sileys. They have no rights under the law. But you and—' He stops to look at the notes on his desk. 'You and Jeremy Tutton have been wrongly reclassified. I can do something about that. And the young girl with you, she's obviously not a Siley. If you cooperate with us, the three of you will be freed.'

'Sorry, then,' I say. 'I've got nothing to add.' I stand up and move towards the door.

'What do you know of what's happening in Wentworth, Finn?' he says to my back. My mind flashes to the two kids we saw playing football, to the way the city glowed when the lights came on tonight. Something pulled at me then, something that promised comfort and warmth.

I turn to face him. 'Not a lot.'

'We're getting back on our feet. Slowly. The virus is still a threat but we're in a better position to cope than at any time in the last three years. We're rebuilding.'

'Using Sileys,' I interrupt.

'We're not perfect, Finn.'

'You don't have to be perfect, just fair.'

He sighs deeply. 'We're feeling our way. It's small steps. We're re-establishing farms, growing food, setting up a society again.'

'A society based on slavery.'

He ignores this comment. 'The truth is, we need people like you and Jeremy. Young people to help us set things right—to lead when the time comes.'

I'm standing between him and the door, weighing what power, if any, I've got in this situation. 'You want me to abandon my friends,' I say finally. 'I can't do that.' I turn towards the door.

'Corporal,' Dowling barks. Winston steps through and blocks my way. He nods back towards Dowling, trying to reassure me.

'Come and sit down,' the general says, his voice sounding tired.

I try to stare him down. The door closes behind me and I walk back to my seat.

'You don't understand the situation,' he continues. 'You are in no position to bargain.'

But I think I am. I've got to use what I know against what he knows. Dad would have called it horsetrading. 'I saw Ramage murder a man,' I say. 'Near Angowrie, two years ago.'

This gets his interest. 'You witnessed it?' he asks.

'Yes. It was a guy called Perkins, one of his own men.' The name sticks in my memory from all that time ago, sitting with Rose at the lookout, after we'd seen Ramage kill him at the hayshed. She said he wasn't all bad. He'd snuck food to the Sileys at the feedstore.

'You saw it happen?' he asks again.

'Yes.'

'And you'd be prepared to make a statement to that affect?'

'Sure. If Kas, Daymu and Ash are released, too. Today.'

'I've told you that's not possible,' he says, but his tone has changed. I'm dangling bait, and he's finding it hard to ignore.

'I can give you more information.' I leave the words hanging there for a few seconds, giving him time to attach weight to them. 'I can point you to someone else here in Wentworth who's seen the worst of Ramage.' I'm thinking of Bridget Monahan. She saw Ramage drag Ken Butler to his death behind a trailbike. And I haven't even got to Kas and JT and what they witnessed at the feedstore.

I feel the balance tip when he breaks eye contact and looks to the ceiling, rubbing his chin with an open hand. He's weighing everything I've said, thinking about the consequences. I've seen the steel in his eyes when he mentions Ramage.

'There's something I want to ask you,' he says, returning to his fatherly tone. 'I know you've had two chances to kill Ramage, but both times you've let him live. Why? If he's a murderer, as you say, why not get rid of him?'

Now I take my time to answer, all the while trying to work out where he's got his information. I'm narrowing it down.

'You know why,' I answer, finally.

He raises his eyebrows. 'Enlighten me,' he says.

'You're holding him captive now, right?'

'Obviously. He's on his way to Wentworth as we speak.'

'So why don't you execute him. I'm sure you could make it happen. You're the law here.'

'Because...' He struggles to find the words.

'Because we're better than that,' I say.

Now he smiles.

'How old are you, Finn?' he asks.

'Seventeen, I think.'

'You've had a tough few years, haven't you?'

My heart burns with the thought of everything I've lost: Mum, Dad, Rose, my home, my life. 'You don't know the half of it,' I say.

'I've got a fair idea.' He shuffles the papers on his desk, looking at one, then another. 'What would you do?' he asks, 'if I allowed you and your friends to—'

'To what?'

'If we came to an agreement for you to give evidence in return for your freedom, would you stay in Wentworth?'

'Are you including Kas and Daymu and Ash?'

He hesitates. 'They couldn't stay here, but maybe—'

'We'd all go back to Angowrie,' I say.

He considers this for a few seconds, looking past me. 'You know that area is under quarantine?' he says.

'Yeah, I've heard that.'

'You'd have no support. We couldn't guarantee your safety outside the fences.'

'The way I see it, you can't guarantee our safety *inside* the fences.'

He sits on this for a while, moving a ring up and down his finger in a way I remember Harry doing. 'And, hypothetically,' he continues, 'if this could be arranged, you'd agree to give evidence against Ramage.'

'Absolutely,' I say.

He nods his head. 'There is something else. You witnessed two other murders. Sergeant Jackson and Jacob Sweeney. They were shot by the rebels.'

I don't say anything.

'So we'd also expect you to make a statement about those crimes. You know who committed them, don't you?'

This is the way deals are made. There's always a catch. He wants me to betray Tahir. 'Sweeney, yes. I didn't see who killed Jackson,' I say. 'But—'

'Sorry, Finn, there are no buts. You'll have to give evidence against the rebels too or we don't have a deal.'

'I need time to think,' I say. 'Besides, you'll never catch them.'

'Maybe. We're short of resources right now, but that won't always be the case. When we do eventually track them down they'll face the full force of the law.'

I've never agreed with Tahir's methods but I understand his motives. On the other hand, I'd also hate to see Gabriel and Afa implicated and maybe my evidence could keep them in the clear.

I try a new tack. 'They have the virus,' I say.

'You mean they're carriers?'

'They have the symptoms. The yellow eyes.'

If I intended this to gain some pity for the No-landers, it

doesn't work. 'This is not an offer I'm going to make again,' Dowling says. 'It's all or nothing. You agree to give evidence against Ramage and the rebels, or the very best I can do is to let you and Jeremy go. The Sileys will continue to work in the abattoir.'

Nothing is ever straightforward—there's always a sting in the tail. The choice is between Kas and Daymu, and Tahir. In the end, it's not a hard decision to make. I nod.

'So that's a yes?' he says.

'Yeah,' I say quietly.

'Thank you, Finn,' he says, and the tension seems to leave his shoulders.

He gets up from behind the desk and sits on the edge again. 'There is no precedent for Sileys being freed. This will have to be a confidential agreement between you and me. And my offer stands—if at any time you and Jeremy want to come back to Wentworth, to help us, you'll be welcome.'

'If the agreement's confidential, what's to stop any new commissioner coming and hunting us again?' I ask. 'If I give evidence, I could make a lot of enemies.'

He smiles. 'Corporal,' he calls and the door opens behind me. 'Bring the new commissioner in.'

Winston closes the door and his boots thump down the corridor.

Dowling sits more easily now. 'We have appointed an interim commissioner, until someone else can be found to replace Ramage.'

He touches my good shoulder and points to the door as it

opens again. Harry stands in front of me, beaming, his whole frame filling the doorway. 'G'day, Finn,' he says.

I can't believe what I'm seeing. *Harry!* Everything that's been building up inside me for weeks—all the hurt and pain and fear—spills out. Tears fill my eyes. I lift myself awkwardly out of the chair and fall into Harry. His big arms hold me and I press my face into his chest. He kisses the top of my head. 'Harry,' I say finally. 'It's so good to see you.'

He directs me back to the chair.

'Willow's here,' I say. 'She's with the others.'

He nods towards the door. Stella walks in, her arm around Willow. Stella's eyes are rimmed red and tears have cut through the grime on Willow's cheeks.

Stella takes my face in her hands. 'Thank you,' she says. 'Thank you, for finding Willow and bringing her back.'

I smile though my own tears. 'Ha,' I say. 'Willow led us here!'

Dowling has returned to his position behind the desk. 'Now,' he says, staring directly at me. 'Do we have a deal?'

I have to pinch myself to make sure this real. 'Yes,' I say, trying to hold myself together. 'We've got a deal.'

He extends his hand and I take it. 'And remember my offer. We need people like you, Finn.'

I nod, but all I can think about at the moment is going home.

'Is there anything else I can do for you?' he asks.

'Yeah, actually, there is. I am really hungry.'

20

Winston leads us down the corridor to a long room lit by two hanging lamps and with a table in the middle. I'm still struggling to get my head around everything that's happened. Harry walks hand-in-hand with Willow, his other arm looped through Stella's. They look healthy, well fed. Stella's hair has grown back—it's sun-bleached and reaches her shoulders. Harry looks more like I remember him from when we first met at Pinchgut Junction. He leans a little to one side when he walks, but other than that you'd never know he was shot last year. They can't wipe the smiles off their faces.

'You took your time to get here, Finn,' Harry says, his voice dry.

'Yeah. I've been a bit busy,' I say.

'What happened to your chin?'

'Cut myself shaving.'

He laughs.

Kas, JT, Daymu and Ash are brought in. Kas rushes at Stella and hugs her.

'So, what's going on?' JT asks. 'Where are the guards?'

'You won't be needing guards,' Harry says.

I tell them about the conversation with Dowling, stringing it out to keep them guessing. When I get to the part about Angowrie, they look at me like I'm bullshitting them.

'You mean—?' Kas says.

'We can go home,' I say.

'*What?*' Her eyes are wide.

Before we know it we're all hugging, forming a big human knot in the middle of the room. Willow reaches up and kisses me on the cheek.

A soldier appears at the door carrying a pile of sandwiches. 'Just Vegemite,' he says apologetically.

'It's okay,' Kas says. 'We can scrape it off. I swear only cockroaches and Vegemite could survive the apocalypse.'

I stand back and look at everyone, lost for words. I can't believe what's happened tonight—the escape from the abattoir, dragging Tusker off the bridge, then thinking we'd blown it all by getting captured. Everything seemed to be stacked against us returning to Angowrie. But now I feel the sea reaching out to me—the rock pools at the point and the beautiful peeling wave at the river mouth. I can almost feel the shock of the saltwater when I first dive under, the way it seems to slide through my body as a wave passes over, and the crusted salt on my skin as I dry in the sun.

Kas is sitting beside me, her legs touching mine, her eyes studying me. 'I know where you are,' she says.

'I'm right here,' I say.

'No, you're not. You're home. You're surfing the river mouth.'

She runs one hand through my hair and kisses me on the lips. 'I can't wait,' she says.

When we've eaten the sandwiches, we're directed to another building, a long hall lined with bunk beds. It's not until I lie down that I realise how exhausted I am. Every muscle aches and my shoulder throbs. I've been given some painkillers and a proper sling to hold my arm but I can only sleep on my back. Kas and I have pulled two mattresses onto the floor so we can lie together. Daymu and JT do the same. Ash is already asleep, and Harry, Stella and Willow are in another room. Kas rests her head on my good shoulder. As tired as I am, sleep doesn't come easily. I keep looking at her to make sure she's real, moving my fingers along her arm to reassure myself. I've missed lying next to her so much: the feeling of her breath on my skin, the way she moulds her body to mine, the warmth she generates.

'I couldn't find Danka,' she whispers. 'No one at the convent remembers her.'

'That could be good news. She might not have been captured.'

'I hope you're right,' she says, but there's sadness in her voice.

'Tell me what happened after we saw you at the courthouse.'

She takes her time to answer, so long I begin to think she's fallen sleep. 'It was awful. The feedstore. Daymu and I were the only ones there and Tusker was...' She stops to draw breath. 'We had to fight him off. It was Ramage who stopped him in the end, when he saw the bruises and cuts. Said we were too valuable to damage, as if we were cattle being prepared for market.'

'Did he...? Were you...?' I can't bring myself to finish the questions.

'No,' she says firmly. 'Daymu and I stuck together the whole time. It was always two against one.'

'How long were you there?'

'We left the day after the trial. I don't think Ramage trusted Tusker to go with us so he sent another Wilder. You remember the guy at the Ramsay farm last year?'

'Col.'

'He was okay. He looked out for us.'

'What happened when you got to Wentworth?'

This time she turns on her side and her lips brush against mine. When she speaks I can feel her breath on my face. 'It wasn't so bad. We got clothes, shoes—and food. Bridget Monahan was in charge. I still don't know what to make of her. She was hard on us. Daymu and me especially, for some reason.'

'She helped us escape,' I say.

'I know, but nothing has changed, Finn. Sileys are always going to be slaves, always treated like shit.'

'Maybe not always.' I'm thinking of my conversation with Dowling. He didn't say it but I got the impression he wasn't comfortable with the treatment of Sileys.

'Did you see what it was like in the abattoir tonight?' Kas says. 'Did you smell it? That's the kind of work Sileys will be doing for years.'

I don't have any arguments to put to her. Change—if it comes at all—will be slow.

She's quiet for a while and I feel her relax into me. She puts her ear to my chest. 'Is it still beating?' I ask.

She gives a choked little laugh that might have tears in it. 'Strong as ever,' she says. She takes my hand and places it over her heart. 'And mine?' she asks.

'Yeah,' I say. 'Like a drum.'

And I realise, for now, this is enough: we have a future to look forward to. It won't be easy, but we'll be together.

Kas's breath deepens and she sleeps.

As tired as I am, I can't sleep. When I close my eyes, the vision of Tusker floating off into the murk of the river appears, his eyes rolling in his head, his mouth open. Everything else that's happened tonight has stopped me thinking about those couple of minutes underwater. Could I have saved him? Pulled him to the surface so at least he had a chance. I hated him with every part of me, but maybe he still deserved that chance. I didn't make a decision like I did with Ramage when I had the opportunity to kill him. This time, I just watched—I allowed him to die. Is that any different from killing someone?

I don't have an answer. I'm too exhausted and I'm going to bed with a full belly, with Kas lying next to me. In time I'll find that answer, but not now. Not here.

*

The next morning there's more food—this time potatoes with bread. I almost made myself sick eating too much last night, so I take it easy. I think my stomach has shrunk with the lack of food.

There are no guards watching us but we've been told not to leave the building.

Harry and Willow arrive as we're eating breakfast. 'How'd you sleep?' Harry asks.

'Okay. What about you?' I say.

'Not so good,' he says. 'Someone kept me awake half the night.'

Stella steps through the door with a child on her hip.

'Hope,' Stella says, looking from her to Kas. 'This is your aunty.'

Kas's mouth opens but no words come out. She moves in slow motion. The last time we saw Hope she was a baby with wispy hair and tiny arms and legs. Now she looks so different. Her features are more defined, her hair is thick and black and her skin is a shade lighter than Kas's. Her eyes—darker even than Rose's—move over us, taking us in.

She lifts her hand to Kas's mouth, then looks back to Stella.

Kas kisses her on the forehead and says, 'Hello, Hope.' She has tears streaming down her cheeks but a wide smile lights her face as she takes Hope into her arms.

Looking at them together like this I can't help but think of Rose. This is the baby she carried to safety, the one she gave her life for, the one she was determined wouldn't be a slave.

And here she is, happy and healthy and safe from the clutches of Ramage.

After breakfast, Kas pulls me to one side. 'We have to speak to Harry,' she says.

'What about?'

'You'll see.'

Harry sits on a bench seat in the morning sun. His back is to the bluestone wall and somehow the harsh light makes him look older, but his face creases into a familiar smile when he sees us.

'What are you two up to?' he asks, shifting to make room on the seat.

Kas leans forward and rests her elbows on her knees, turning sideways to look at Harry.

'Harry,' she starts, and I can see her struggling with whatever the question is she wants to ask. She flicks a glance at me before continuing. I don't know where she's going but she wants my support. 'The Sileys,' she says, finally. 'If you're the commissioner, you'll be responsible for hunting them down, capturing them.'

It doesn't sound like an accusation, but there's intent in her words.

Harry exhales, like he's been holding his breath. 'I wondered how long it would take you to ask,' he says.

Kas nods. 'So...I'm asking now.'

I've never taken the time to think about Kas's relationship to Harry. Now that I do, it seems she gravitates towards Stella and Willow, as though there's something about Harry she doesn't quite get. Maybe it's his understated way of doing things, or how the gaps he leaves in conversations sometimes carry more meaning than the words. And I haven't forgotten she was a prisoner at the valley farm when Harry was in charge. She sussed out Tusker pretty quickly, but Harry must have puzzled her—an honest man who, nonetheless, exploited Sileys.

'To be honest, Kas. I don't know what's going to happen. But Dowling wants to change the way things are done in the zones. I told him I'm only interested in the job if I can concentrate on farming and rebuilding the community.'

'And the bounty hunters?' Kas persists.

'Every hunter is one less farmer.' He's been avoiding Kas's gaze but now he turns to her. He gently places his hand on her shoulder. 'I'll do everything I can, Kas. I promise.'

Kas looks like she wants to push him further, but she leans back against the wall, her head tilted to the sky. Harry's hand stays on her shoulder, asking a question in its own way. Finally, she nods.

Winston strides across the yard with Daymu, JT and Ash. 'We need to go to the medical room,' he says.

This is done secretly, via back corridors in the jail. We move quickly, and Winston tells us to not to talk. He hustles us into a bright room, which he quickly darkens by drawing the curtains.

'Why all the sneaking around?' Daymu asks.

'The fewer people that see you the better,' Winston says. 'We still haven't worked out how we're going to get you outside the fences.' He pauses. 'Not you two,' he says nodding at JT and me. 'Just the—'

'Sileys.' Daymu completes the sentence for him.

'You have to understand the risk Dowling is taking,' Winston says. 'This has never been done before.'

The door opens and a figure is silhouetted in the light from the corridor.

'So, we meet again,' a woman's voice says.

It's Angela, the doctor from Longley. I know the risk she took for us, and I'm relieved she's still free. She puts out her hand and I shake it.

'Hey,' I say. 'It's good to see you.'

'You look like shit,' she says. 'What have they done to you?' She lifts my chin with her finger and checks the cut. 'You haven't looked after those stitches either.'

'Not really my fault,' I say.

'And your shoulder?'

'Dislocated yesterday. JT put it back in.'

She carefully eases me out of the sling. 'Not a bad job,' she says. 'Bet it hurt, though.'

She looks at us, checking our eyes first. Then she notes the trackers on our left hands. 'Looks like I've got some work to do,' she says, opening a drawer and laying out instruments on a small table.

She cleans my chin first then gives my shoulder a gentle workout to check the range of movement. 'Keep it in the sling for a couple of weeks,' she says.

Angela takes blood from all of us, labelling the samples as she goes. 'I'm only guessing at Dowling's plans for you, but you'd better pray these tests come back negative.'

'What about the tests you did on JT and me in Longley?' I ask.

'Negative,' she replies. 'But you've been out in the wild again since then.'

I tell her about Gabriel.

'That's not good news,' she says. 'If you are heading outside the fences, you'll always be at risk.'

'Seems to me there's risk everywhere—unless they've worked out how to stop the wind blowing.'

The last thing she does is remove our trackers. She starts with Kas, making a small slit in the skin close to her wrist, then sliding a narrow probe through the gap until it contacts the device. 'This disarms it,' she says. 'And retracts the wires that hold it in place.'

Finally, she pulls the little piece of black metal free with a pair of tweezers. She holds it up to Kas's face. 'There,' she says. 'You're officially no longer a Siley.'

Kas bites her bottom lip. I know she's thinking of Rose. It was the infection that developed after she removed her tracker that killed her.

One by one, Angela extracts our devices, finishing each job with two small stitches I can hardly see. While she works she talks. 'They found a body down river this morning,' she says. 'It was Tusker.' She looks at me. 'Seems he fell off a bridge.'

I shrug my shoulders.

A faint smile crosses her lips, then disappears. 'He went rogue when they arrested Ramage.'

'No one's going to grieve for him,' Kas says, her voice hard.

Angela stops what she's doing. 'You know they're bringing Ramage here today?'

It's mid-afternoon, hot and windy with dust swirling in the air, when a truck passes through the gates, surrounded by soldiers on foot, all armed and on alert. The truck swings around and backs up to one end of the courtyard. Kas and I watch from a window no more than ten metres away. The tailgate drops and Ramage emerges, shading his eyes from the sun.

Somehow, he looks older than when we saw him at the trial in Longley, like he's shrunk. His shoulders hunch and he keeps his gaze to the ground. It's only when they lift him down that I see his ankles are chained together, forcing him to shuffle.

Dowling steps into the courtyard and stands in front of Ramage, who finally raises his head. His stubble is patchy and grey and his hair is plastered with sweat. Dowling says something to him and he shakes his head slowly. Even from this distance I can see the contempt on his face. Dowling steps aside and the guard pushes Ramage through the door and out of sight.

Kas has been holding my hand, squeezing it tight while we've watched this little exchange.

'Do you think he's Hope's father?' I ask.

She turns to me, the question surprising her. She pauses, considering her answer. Slowly, she nods. 'Once he found out Rose was pregnant,' she says, 'he stopped her going out to work on the farms and made sure she had enough to eat.'

'Do you think he loved her?' I ask.

Again, she takes her time to answer. 'No,' she says, finally. 'It can't be love when the other person hates you.'

After the lights come on that night, Winston takes me to a bright room with a table and two chairs. Dowling joins us and sits opposite me.

'Did you see Ramage arrive today?' he says, his voice low and serious.

'Yes.'

'You need to write down everything you can remember about the murder you witnessed. Then you can sign it as a sworn statement.'

'Will I still have to appear in court?'

'No. The statement will be enough,' he says.

I don't know how I feel about this. A part of me wants to confront Ramage, to see him when he faces the charges, but another part of me wants to get back to the coast as soon as I can.

'Is it a real court?' I ask.

'It's the best we can do at the moment.'

'What happens if he's not found guilty?'

'Don't worry. We have enough evidence. The punishment will be up to me to decide.' He leaves it at that and I'm left to wonder how they'll deal with people like Ramage in this new world they're building.

I've told Dowling about Bridget Monahan and what she saw Ramage do to Ken Butler. Winston reckons she's only too happy to give evidence. It looks like I won't need to mention Kas and JT.

'Take your time,' Dowling says, walking out of the room with Winston. 'Don't omit any detail.'

Trying to recall everything Rose and I saw that day at the hayshed is like opening a book I haven't read for ages—I have to find the story again, to figure where it fits with everything else that was happening back then.

There are a few things I remember easily because they shocked me: Rose wearing one of Mum's dresses when I came back from hunting that morning; her changing the bandages on her hand and seeing the wariness in her eyes when I tried to help; I remember sitting on the ridge and looking out to sea, her telling me how weird it was when she saw me surfing. And slowly, my mind creeps through the bracken fern and climbs the tree to look at the Wilder's camp at the hayshed. I can still feel the rough bark against my chest where we lay on the branches.

Ramage attacked Perkins with a spear, stabbing him again and again, and the Wilder's body jerked up and down with every blow. I remember Rose touching my hand and turning away. And then Ramage pulled the dead man's boots off and walked away, leaving him lying in the paddock.

I put it all down, trying not to get caught up in the fear and anger. I haven't written anything in three years and my handwriting is scratchy, like it's hard to form the letters. When I finish, I'm exhausted.

Dowling returns, takes the paper and reads it slowly, nodding his head. Every now and again he makes a *tsk tsk* sound with his tongue. Finally, he lays it on the table and looks at me.

'Shocking,' he says.

'Is it enough?' I ask.

'It'll do. With Bridget Monahan's evidence, we should have enough to convict him. But now, I need you to recount everything you saw when Sweeney was murdered.'

This memory is much fresher, and it takes me no time to describe. There are some things I can't put into words—the thud of the bullet into his chest, the way his body slumped to the ground, Tahir's shrug and the ripple of fear that ran through everyone watching.

This time Dowling stays in the room. He studies me long and hard and my stomach squirms at the thought of him going back on our deal.

When I'm done, I ask if we can go home now.

'As soon as we get your blood tests back,' he says.

'There's one more thing I want to do,' I say.

'What's that?'

'I want to see Ramage.'

Dowling doesn't reply straightaway. He's weighing me up again. Finally, he nods. 'Wait here,' he says, stepping outside to talk to Winston, who throws me a disbelieving look.

A few minutes later Ramage arrives with two guards. The chains have been taken off his ankles but he still shuffles like an old man. He is pushed into the chair opposite me.

'Do you want me to stay?' Dowling asks.

'No.'

'I'll be right outside,' he says.

I'm left with Ramage, who sits with his elbows on the table and his fingers woven together. His breathing is laboured, and

222

all his movements are slow and deliberate, as though he has to convince his body to make them. His face shows nothing. His eyes are glazed and he blinks in the hard light. One shoulder sits uncomfortably lower than the other.

It's a surreal moment, sitting opposite this man I've feared and hated in equal amounts. He's responsible for Rose's death, for all the abuse at the feedstore, for the enslaving of the valley farmers, for the horrible murder of Ken Butler.

He scratches at the stubble on his chin and says, 'What've you got to say, kid? I'm all ears.'

'Not much,' I say, feeling my stomach tighten. 'I just wanted you to know—'

'You're giving evidence against me,' he interrupts. 'I know. They told me. You and that Monahan bitch.'

I try to focus on all the things I should say to him, everything that's been building up since Rose arrived on the beach in Angowrie. But the words are lost somewhere and I start to wonder if this is actually a good idea.

He sits back in his chair and crosses his arms. 'I know what you think of me, Finn. But the world was falling apart and someone had to step up to the plate and lead. I had to be hard—it just couldn't be done any other way. I saved our little part of the world and this is the thanks I get.' He waves his arms at the four walls. 'But this isn't the end of it. There'll be someone to fill the gap I leave, you wait and see.'

He stops then and his face softens, like a burden has been lifted off his shoulders; as though he'd always expected it would end like this.

'You think I hate you, Finn, but I don't.'

Something crawls under my skin every time he uses my name.

He continues. 'We'd have made a good team, you and me. You could have trimmed some of the hardness off me. Pulled me back on some of my'—he struggles to find the word—'my excesses.'

It's like he finds his way into my head when he talks, not allowing me space to think. This isn't what I was expecting. I don't want to hear his justifications. I don't want to know what he thinks of me.

My heart is hammering in my chest.

It's Dad who saves me, his voice coming to me from days we spent bobbing in the water, waiting between sets at the river mouth. *Be patient*, he'd say. *Don't chase the waves, hold your spot and when the time is right, take control. Seize the moment, Finn. When it's your time.*

My breathing slows and the words come without me having to think. 'You didn't step up to the plate, you just made things worse. What you did to the Sileys, to the feedstore kids, that wasn't leadership, it was abuse. You did it because you could, because there was no one to stop you. You know what Rose told me?'

I know Rose is my way through to him. His eyes meet mine.

'She told me she hated you more than anyone on Earth. She ran away because she loathed you and she didn't want her baby to be a slave. You drove her to her death.'

He tries to act as though this doesn't affect him but his twitching lip gives him away. The tension returns to his shoulders and he squares himself in the chair. I see his move before he's even thought of it. His hand slips below the table and he lurches out of his chair gripping a knife. He's slow though. I spring back as he throws his body at me, the knife in his right hand just missing me. I'm so much quicker than him, even with one arm in a sling. I knock the knife away and grab him by the hair, forcing his face into the tabletop. He groans and pushes back.

Dowling and the guards storm into the room. Ramage swings his arms wildly as he tries to fend them off. But, whatever strength he once had, it's deserted him now. His arm is wrenched up his back and he's forced upright.

'I heard about Tusker,' he yells, spit flying from his mouth. 'I know what you did. We're the same, you and me.'

21

From the ridge, Angowrie looks exactly as I left it: the houses hunkered down in the tea trees and moonah, the river snaking its way out to the beach, the rocky point and the deep blue of the ocean beyond. Inside the bay, the sea sparkles in the morning light, and I inhale the smell of home. The first, faint sign of autumn is on the breeze, a coolness that means the winds will soon begin to push in from the west. The currents will shift, bringing colder water from down south and early storms will brew in the bight.

Today has been such a rush. We were woken before dawn and hustled out into the courtyard where a truck was idling.

I assume our blood tests came back negative and that's why we were free to go.

Harry, Stella and Willow were in the yard, waiting for us. Harry was holding Hope.

'It seems we're always saying goodbye to you two,' Stella said. The air was cold enough for steam to form as we breathed. She kissed us quickly and Harry passed Hope to us. She was still sleepy and as soon as she felt the warmth of Kas's body she rested her head into her shoulder. Kas whispered in her ear, then reluctantly handed her back to Stella.

'Come and visit us in the valley,' Harry said quietly.

The rules of our release don't allow for travel outside the quarantine zone, but one day we'd make it happen. 'We will,' I said.

Seeing Willow with her parents reminded me of how young she is. She seemed so much older when she'd been travelling with us. She hugged Kas and me long and hard. 'Don't forget me,' she said, hanging onto us until the last minute.

'How could I forget my sister,' I said.

Winston hurried us into the back of the truck. It was stacked with boxes and bags of seed. Some of this was for us but most was going to Longley. We slid into a small gap between the cargo and the cabin and pulled a tarp over the top. Our last glimpse of Harry, Stella, Willow and Hope was of them pressed together against the cold. Willow broke away as we passed through the gates and ran behind us, her arms waving wildly in the air.

The morning chill found its way under the tarp, but with

five of us in there, body heat kept us warm. I'm sure we all had the same look in our eyes—disbelief that this was actually happening. Three checkpoints stood between us and freedom and none of us would relax until we were through them.

The first checkpoint was at the wire fence. The truck pulled to a halt and we heard Winston declare a delivery of farm supplies to Longley. The flap was lifted for a few seconds then dropped again. The gates scraped open and we passed through slowly. Winston zigzagged through the bollards protecting the gate, then we picked up speed.

Having been allowed through this gate, we were waved through the second one. The last checkpoint was at the fence where we first met Ash. This time the motor was turned off and someone heaved themselves into the tray. We huddled together, not daring to breathe. We could hear someone poking at the seed bags and boxes.

Winston must have climbed up with the guard.

'This is a lot of stuff for Longley,' the guard said. I could hear the suspicion in his voice.

'Payment for the last load of Sileys,' Winston said.

'Do you know anything about the escapees?' the guard asked.

'At the abattoir, you mean? All rounded up.' Winston was trying to sound casual.

Footsteps moved closer and something hit a box close to our heads. 'What's behind here?' the guard asked.

Kas tensed next to me. We were ready to fight if we had to.

'I told you, it's supplies for Longley,' Winston said, his voice sharp. 'You want to tell General Dowling you held up his shipment?'

'Dowling? Why didn't you say so?'

The next sound was of boots hitting the asphalt road and the guard calling, 'All good here.'

As we moved away from the gate and the truck slowly climbed the hill, we crawled out of our hiding spot and began to relax. Once we were out of sight of the guards, we lifted the flap and allowed the morning sun to shine in under the canopy.

A pack of mangy dogs appeared, barking wildly and snapping at the tyres. One by one they dropped off until only a single dog tried to keep up the pretense of a chase. Soon it was lost in the dust thrown up from the road.

After ten minutes we pulled over next to a line of pine trees and Winston appeared at the back. 'Everyone okay?' he asked.

We took the chance to spread out and have a piss. When I walked back to the truck Kas was standing in the middle of the road, her hands on her head and her eyes closed. She was breathing deeply.

'What's up?' I asked.

There were tears in her eyes. 'Hope won't remember me,' she said. 'She'll grow up thinking Stella and Harry are her parents.'

I put my arms around her. 'We'll get to the valley somehow. I promised Harry.'

Winston climbed back into the cabin. 'Come on, we've gotta get going,' he called. 'We'll turn off for the coast soon. Stick to the back roads.'

'Wait!' Kas yelled. She'd been climbing the tailgate but now she hurried to the front of the tray and banged on the cabin. She grabbed me by the hand and pulled me to the open flap. We were looking directly into the sun but I could hear barking.

A lone dog appeared out of the morning glare, the last one from the pack that tried to chase us.

It was Rowdy. I jumped onto the road and he ran into me like he hadn't seen me. He was limping badly and his coat was a mess of cuts and sores. It looked like he had been in a fight. I hugged him and lifted him into Kas's arms. Winston was already on the move, the truck lurching as he picked up speed. I scrambled aboard. We found a hessian bag and wrapped Rowdy in it. His body was shaking but he settled once he felt me there with him. I held him close and he licked at my arm.

We followed the highway for another ten minutes before turning south along a dirt track, leaving the flat of the plain and entering the stringybark woodland. We had to stop a dozen times to move branches and debris out of our way, but eventually we swung back to the coast road that had been cleared by the truck Tusker took to Angowrie. Flashes of abandoned houses and farms triggered memories of bus trips to school before the virus. That seemed a lifetime ago.

Eventually the land levelled out as we drove west, parallel to the coast. As we passed the top of the Addiscot Valley, I tried to make out the track down to Ray's old place, but everything was different, the bush had closed in on any open space. We slowed at the intersection with the road to Pinchgut Junction and I could sense home. A couple of minutes later, we thumped on the cabin and got Winston to pull over. We were on the ridge, overlooking town.

'So, this is Angowrie,' Ash says. He holds Daymu's hand and I'm sure they are thinking the same as me—that it's beautiful, but isolated. With all the excitement of coming home, I haven't forgotten we'll need to work hard to survive here. The virus will always be a threat. We can protect ourselves against drifters, No-landers and even rogue Wilders if it comes to that, but the virus can arrive at any time, invisible and deadly.

We descend the hill to the bridge, cross without stopping and pull up on the riverbank where the Wilders camped two years ago. I climb onto the roof and whistle as loud as I can, followed by the wattlebird call. I stop and listen but all that comes to me is the sound of the wind and the background roar of the surf.

'If Ray's in the house on the hill, he might not hear you,' Kas says. She reaches into the cabin and leans on the horn. The blast echoes up the valley.

'Let's drive there,' JT says but he barely gets the words out before we see a figure moving under the trees in the house opposite. We take cover behind the truck as Winston draws the gun from his belt.

'Who are you?' It's a girl's voice, wary and scared.

Kas gives a little squeal and takes off across the road, hurdling the fence and launching herself at the girl. She calls over her shoulder, 'It's Danka!'

Danka breaks away from Kas and greets Daymu, JT and

me with big hugs. She has a bandage around her left hand.

'I can't believe it,' Danka says. There are tears running down her cheeks. 'How—?'

'It's a long story,' I say. 'But what about you? How did you get here?'

'That's another long story,' she says.

'Where's Ray?'

She drops her eyes and the smile leaves her face. 'In your old place,' she says, quietly. 'He's not good.'

'We have to unload,' Winston interrupts. 'I've got to get to Longley by midday or it'll look suspicious.'

'I'll direct him up the street,' Danka says. 'You go see Ray.'

All the familiarity of home reaches out to me as we walk up the street from the river. The trees seem to have closed in over the road, and weeds have almost covered the bitumen. We move quickly down the driveway and into the backyard. Rowdy limps along next to us.

Ray is in bed with his head propped on a couple of pillows. His hair is thinner and greyer than I remember, almost white, and it looks like he hasn't shaved in weeks. His body seems to have sunk under the weight of the blankets. He opens his eyes when he hears us, taking time to focus. 'That you, Danka?' he says, his voice soft and croaky.

Kas and I sit on the bed, either side of him. She gently pushes the hair off his face. 'It's Kas and Finn, Ray. We've come home.'

He takes a moment to process this. 'Finn?' he says. His chest wheezes as he speaks. 'And Kas? Ah, it's so good to see you.' He lifts both his hands and we take them in ours. His skin is thin and dry like paper. 'I've been a bit crook,' he says.

'You'll be fine,' Kas says. 'We're all here to help. JT and Daymu, Danka—we'll get you well.'

He forces a smile and his thumb rubs the top of my hand. 'I've been waiting for you,' he says, his voice a whisper now. 'Thought those bastards had caught you again.'

'We'll tell you everything later,' I say.

'It doesn't matter, son. None of it matters. You're home.' His eyes close and his breath deepens. 'Bit tired,' he murmurs.

We slip out of the room and find the others in the kitchen. Daymu and JT sit at the table with Ash, and Danka stands by the door.

'How long's he been like this?' I ask Danka.

'Since I got here, about a week ago,' she says. 'I was going door to door, trying to find this place. He'd had a fall in the backyard. It took me ages to get him cleaned up and into bed. He hasn't eaten.'

Kas hugs her. 'You did well,' she says.

'Have his eyes been sore at all?' I ask Danka.

'No. Why?'

I explain the symptoms of the new strain of the virus.

'It's not the virus, Finn,' she says. 'It's old age and a tough life.'

'Has he spoken much to you?' I ask.

'Only bits and pieces,' Danka says. 'He said he saw a truck pass through the day after you left. Then the decontamination squad came. He hid in a place up on the hill until they left. Then he tried to get back down here.'

We're interrupted by the sound of the truck backing into the driveway. 'Come on,' JT says, 'we need to get this stuff stored away.'

There's tinned food, powdered milk, vegetable seeds, medical supplies and even some tea. And there's a rifle and ammo.

Ash has been quiet since we arrived, taking everything in, trying to figure out where Ray and Danka fit into our story. His eyes widen at the sight of the gas bottles and supplies in the garage.

By the time we've unloaded, the shelves are almost full. Winston is ready to leave but we've got a decision to make. I go into Ray's room and touch his arm to wake him. He seems confused, but gradually focuses on my face. He forces a smile. 'What now?' he says.

I explain about the truck—how he could get to a doctor in Longley. He's shaking his head before I even finish.

'No, Finn,' he says. 'Everything I need is here.'

'But we can't make you better,' I argue.

'No one can, son.'

My heart's not in the argument, but I press on. 'You'd be more comfortable in a hospital,' I say.

Now he takes my hand and squeezes it. 'I don't want to die in a hospital, Finn. I'm content here—with my family.'

That word breaks me up. We are a family and we need to look after each other.

I nod and his eyes close again. The conversation has exhausted him.

We say our goodbyes to Winston and walk out to the river-bank to watch the truck labour up the hill and out of town.

The smell of diesel hovers in the air for a while then disappears on the breeze.

The days roll into each other and we establish a routine of looking after Ray, hunting, fishing and tending the vegetable gardens we've planted with the seed Dowling gave us. It's late in the season, but we hope to get some lettuce, rhubarb and onions growing before the autumn gets too cold. Rowdy is recovering and has put some meat back on his bones. My shoulder is improving but I'm still wearing the sling so I'm pretty limited in what I can do. JT and Daymu have proved good hunters with the rifle. There are plenty of kangaroos and wallabies around. My stomach is readjusting to regular meals and we're all starting to look healthier. Each day we split the chores and decide who'll be on sentry duty. For the time being we have the town to ourselves, but we keep watch anyway—we don't know who might be surviving outside the fences.

Ray is wasting away before our eyes—he goes days without speaking or eating. Danka is his main carer—they became close when they were here on their own. She helps out with other chores when she can, but mostly she spends her time looking after him. She tries to spoonfeed him and keep him hydrated, but it's like he's willing himself to let go.

Kas and I sit with Ray most evenings, talking and reading to him, even though he's usually asleep.

Later, we crawl into bed exhausted from the day's work. Our bodies fall into each other and I drift off with her breath on my neck.

I sleep differently at home. I don't start awake, thinking there'll be someone with a knife at my throat. I don't dream of the thrum of a trailbike or the metallic sound of the bolt being shifted on a rifle. If I wake before Kas, I lie and look at her. She moves her lips in her sleep, like she's having a conversation with someone in her dreams. Somehow, she always senses me watching and her eyes open, focus slowly and crease at the edges knowing she's landed somewhere permanent at last—or as permanent as anything can be in this new version of the world.

Days pass and Ray drifts in and out of consciousness. Last night was like any other. We sat on his bed, and talked about the weather changing, the shift in the winds and the progress of our vegetables. Outside, the cypress branches brushed against the guttering and the sheoaks moaned. Rowdy snored loudly in the kitchen. I like to think these were the last things he heard, the comfortable and familiar sounds of home. I hope he didn't wake in the night, afraid. I hope he was thinking about Harriet and the life they had on the farm before the virus.

When the candle flickered and spluttered out, throwing us into darkness, Kas and I made our way to our room, thinking he'd still be there in the morning. I wish now I had stayed longer, held his hand and told him I loved him. I wish I'd been there when he took his last breath. But that only happens in the movies—it's not the way death arrives at all. It comes in the night, hopefully in the depths of sleep when a dream melts into something else, something quiet and peaceful, and that last breath is an easy one to let go of. That's how I like to think of Ray passing.

22

After the tears, the hugs and the stories, we all agree Ray should be buried on his own land. Danka offers to prepare him for the trip while the rest of us go about making a cart we can carry him on.

Two days later, our little procession sets out. Ray's body is wrapped in a sheet and we secure him to the flatbed top of the cart. Ash has volunteered to stay in Angowrie with Rowdy to watch the house and supplies.

The breeze has picked up off the strait but the sun is out and the last of the fruit trees around town are dropping their leaves. It must be May. I remember it being like this, the warmth holding on through the day and the winter reaching out at night. We take it in turns to push Ray on his last journey out to the farm. I wonder how many times he drove this road, heading into Angowrie with Harriet to do the shopping and fill the car with petrol. Maybe he stopped off at the hardware and chatted to the bloke that ran it. Maybe I brushed past him when I was working there on a Saturday morning. Maybe he tousled my hair and asked me how school was going.

It takes us a couple of hours to reach the top of the valley. It's my first day out of the sling, but I'm determined to play my part in giving Ray the send-off he deserves. The going gets tough when we turn down the rough track towards the farm. It's overgrown with hakea and prickly mimosa and we have to lift the cart over fallen branches. Finally we reach the gate to the home paddock, where the valley opens out and gives us a clear view down to Red Rocks and the ocean.

Kas stops inside the gate and looks along the fence line. 'We should bury him next to Rose,' she says.

I go to get a spade from the shed. The grass has begun to reclaim the ruins of Ray's house, the long grass runners snaking through the blackened timbers and roofing iron. A shudder passes through me when I think of everything that happened here: Hope being born, Rose dying, the house burning to the ground, and Kas killing the two Wilders at the shed. I don't dare look to see if their remains are still there. I grab a spade and hurry back up the paddock. The afternoon is wearing on and we've got a lot of digging to do.

It takes the best part of two hours to dig the grave. My

shoulder is weak but somehow the pain feels good, like it should hurt to bury someone you love. We take it in turns, resting against the fence in between, though JT and Danka do most of the work. In between turns with the spade, Kas cleans up around Rose's grave.

The sun is low by the time we've finally got the hole deep enough. Sea mist rolls up the valley and, all through the bush behind us, birds sing. A mob of kangaroos has found its way through gaps in the boundary fence to graze in the open paddock.

We ease Ray into the grave, then shovel and push the dirt in on top of him until the hole is filled. All the digging and sweating has been a distraction, but now there's time to stop and let it sink in. The last of the sun filters through the stringy-barks, giving the mist a warm glow. We stand in silence for a while, Kas holding my hand, Danka, JT and Daymu leaning into each other.

'You knew him best,' Kas says to me. 'You should say something.'

You'd reckon I'd know a bit about grief by now, losing Dad and Mum and Rose. But it still strangles the breath out of me, pulling at me, trying to confuse my thoughts. Just crying and leaving it at that would be easy, but Ray deserves more so I wipe away the tears and search for the right words.

'First time I saw Ray after the virus was over at that fence,' I begin, pointing to where the kangaroos came into the paddock. 'He told me to bugger off!'

The others smile.

'But that was Ray—tough on the outside, kind and gentle on the inside. I wouldn't have made it through that first winter without him. He saved me, and he never asked for anything in return. He did everything he could to help Rose and Hope.'

Kas has looped her arm around my waist and now she squeezes me closer.

'Somehow, with the virus, and everything that came with it, Ray stayed the same—straight-up, no bullshit, always there to lend a hand or say the right thing when you needed it most. Thanks for being our friend, Ray. And thanks for taking our side when no one else was there to help. We love you. Rest in peace.'

Autumn creeps towards winter—the days are getting shorter and the nights cooler. We haven't had any big storms yet, but it's only a matter of time. It'll be tough when they come, limiting our hunting options and forcing us to rely more on our stores. We've reinforced the house as best we can to prepare for the battering it'll take when the weather turns. JT and Daymu have been up on the roof, double nailing the corrugated iron, while the rest of us have scoured the town to find shutters for the windows.

There's a hole in every day where Ray used to be. His chair at the kitchen table is empty, and when I go to the store for supplies, my heart aches at the sight of his lists, written in that familiar scrawl and pinned to the wall. I keep thinking I'll walk out into the yard and find him propped in his usual spot against the shed wall, his arms and legs covered against the sun, his hands working grease into the springs of a rabbit trap. Last summer, when it was just Kas and me here with him, he always found something to do, even when we were relaxing—tending to the garden, pumping water into the header tank or laying out our weekly provisions from the store. Life was work for him—he didn't know any other way. Mostly I miss his voice. I miss the way he called me son and the blokey conversations we'd have, talking rubbish and never saying what we meant.

Rowdy misses him, too. He still sniffs around Ray's room and follows his scent out to the shed. He'll sit by Ray's chair in the sun, waiting for him to come down the stairs on those bowed legs, take a seat with a pot of potatoes to peel and reach down to scratch his ears.

It's a windless day and the sun still has some warmth in it. Kas and I are sitting on the bench at the lookout. My eyes are drawn to the break at the river mouth. It's a small swell but the waves wrap themselves around the bar and I surf them in my mind: taking the drop and bottom-turning into the steep section, looking for a little cover-up before shooting out onto the open wall. I can almost feel the spray at my back.

'Hey,' Kas says, snapping her fingers in front of my face. 'Remember me?'

Her face glows in the afternoon light. Her thick hair is tucked behind her ears and her knees are pulled up to her chest. Her skin is cool where our shoulders touch. She picks at the scab on the back of her hand. We've hardly spoken about what the future holds for us. There are no guarantees the virus won't find us. In some ways though, it forces us to live for every moment, to hang on to days like this, knowing they're precious.

The one thing Kas has decided is she's going to search along the coast for Yogi and Bess. She reckons they'll have found feed in a paddock somewhere this side of Devils Elbow.

We've settled back into a comfortable routine. Angowrie is our home in the way nowhere else could be. We're connected to this place—to every grain of sand, to the twisted boughs of the tea trees and the smell of the moonahs after rain. To the pigface that clings to the dunes where nothing else will grow. We breathe the salt air into our lungs, and it spreads through every artery and vein.

Out at sea, a storm is brewing and we watch it push away to the east, rumbling and dark, but small, with one steeple of coal-black cloud and blue sky either side. It's shot through with the arc of a rainbow.

'This is where it all began,' I say. 'When Rose ran onto the beach. I remember the look in her eyes and even what she was wearing—baggy shorts and a way-too-big jumper. And she swam like a fish when we jumped in the river to escape.'

Kas stares at the horizon but I feel her edge closer. 'What was the first thing she said?' she asks.

'*You gotta help me.*'

'And you did.'

'Yeah, I did.'

We sit with this for a while before Kas gets to her feet and leans in to kiss me. 'We should make the most of the sun while it's still here,' she says.

She jumps off the platform and follows the track leading to the beach. Halfway down she turns and looks at me.

'Come on,' she calls.

I haven't tested my shoulder in the surf yet, and it still aches from the digging when we buried Ray. Now I roll it in half-circles. It catches a little but feels okay.

Below me, Kas hurls herself at the white water and lets out a squeal.

I run down to join her.

ACKNOWLEDGMENTS

A heartfelt thank you to all the people who have invested their time and energy in the Winter series, in particular my first readers, Lynne Batson, Nicole Maher and Kerrie Sirotich. Thanks to Lynne, for looking at the first raw draft and letting me know I was on the right track. Thanks to Kerrie for highlighting the gaps in the narrative and yet still being supportive and affirming.

To Nicole, special thanks for casting a discerning professional eye over later drafts and making so many constructive suggestions for improvements. You are every writer's dream—a ruthlessly honest critic and friend whose love of reading and writing shines through. I can't thank you enough for the support you have given me from the beginning.

To my young readers, Matilda and Harriet Lohrey, thank you for your comments, suggestions and ideas—and for not being afraid to tell your uncle when he was getting off-track or missing an important point.

To Jason and Anna for the use of my writing home-away-from-home at Falmouth. Every writer should be so lucky as to have supportive family and friends with houses in beautiful places.

To the whole crew at Text who believed in the Winter series from the beginning. Thanks to Michael Heyward for your passion for publishing Australian writers, to Imogen Stubbs for another stunning cover, to Shalini Kunahlan and the marketing team for leaving no stone unturned in getting my books into the public eye, and to Jamila Khodja for managing the publicity so efficiently.

To Jane Pearson, who manages to make my books infinitely better than they otherwise would be. You are patient, encouraging and professional on every level. You know when to push hard and when to let things pass through to the keeper.

To my writing network (from all genres), I am blessed to have so many creative and supportive friends among the writing community. To the staff and leadership team at St Bernard's for their support and for allowing me the time away from regular duties to promote my books.

And finally, to my family, near and extended, for coming along for the ride. To June Monica, for her enduring love and support—and for imbuing in me a love of reading and writing. To Oliver, Maddy and Harley for being the most loving, honest and supportive (in the very best taking-the-piss fashion) human beings a father could hope for.

And to Lynne. Because you're the one.